Charlotte Mary Yonge

The Pilgrimage of the Ben Beriah

Charlotte Mary Yonge

The Pilgrimage of the Ben Beriah

ISBN/EAN: 9783337288082

Printed in Europe, USA, Canada, Australia, Japan

Cover: Foto ©Andreas Hilbeck / pixelio.de

More available books at **www.hansebooks.com**

THE PILGRIMAGE OF
THE BEN BERIAH

THE PILGRIMAGE

OF

THE BEN BERIAH

BY

CHARLOTTE M. YONGE

London

MACMILLAN AND CO., LIMITED

NEW YORK: THE MACMILLAN COMPANY

1899

So when at last our weary days
  Are well-nigh wasted here,
And we can trace God's ' wondrous ways '
  In distance calm and clear ;

When in His love and Israel's sin
  We read our story true,
We may not, all too late, begin
  To wish our hopes were new.

KEBLE.

CONTENTS

PART I

CHAPTER I

CHAPTER VI

CHAPTER VII

CHAPTER VIII

CHAPTER IX

CHAPTER X

CHAPTER XI

CHAPTER XII

CHAPTER XIII

CHAPTER XIV

CHAPTER XV

CHAPTER XVI

CHAPTER XVII

CHAPTER XVIII

CHAPTER XIX

PAGE

CHAPTER XX

PART II

CHAPTER I

CHAPTER II

CHAPTER III

CHAPTER IV

CHAPTER V

CHAPTER VI

CHAPTER VII

CHAPTER VIII

ILLUSTRATIONS

PART I

B

CHAPTER I

THE EVENING OF HOPE

Far through that solemn eve the young lambs dying
Had bleated out their sweet lives while they bled,
  As a child sings itself to sleep with crying.
By every hearth the victim blood was shed,
On every board the hasty feast was spread.
                                        MRS. ALEXANDER.

THE red cloudless sun was setting over the cornfields of the land of Goshen, as they lay green and beginning to form their ears for the coming harvest time. The light was reflected in the stream of the Nile, and sparkled again and again in the lesser canals that irrigated the country, and whose banks of mud divided the small gardens, where luxuriant gourds, dourra, a grain like rice, and other vegetables were beginning to grow, watered by the machine attached to each garden, by which a vessel was fastened to a kind of yoke, belonging to a pole, with a weight at the other end. A man drew the water up and dispensed it to the fertile but thirsty soil, but charily, for the river was getting low and the beneficent inundation would not come quickly.

In the garden, with pitcher on her head, stood a girl of about fourteen or fifteen. The evening light bathed the coarse blue pitcher on her head and the beautiful face under it, as well as the dark blue garment in which she was wrapped, excepting her slender young arms and bare feet. Her long black hair was plaited in tight formal tresses, hanging down so as to frame her lovely young brown face, clear, but with rosy colour in the cheeks and lips. Round her were flying doves, white or purple, one perched on the edge of her pitcher, another on her shoulder, their rainbow necks glistening changeably in the sun. But it was not to their cooings that she was attending, her great soft dark eyes were fixed on the evening distance, and the reflected light in the river. 'It is even as it was when the water was changed to blood,' she murmured to herself. 'That was when first the promises of our deliverance came to us! O God of our Fathers, set us free!'

'How long must we tarry?' cried another dark maiden, who had come up with her pitcher. 'Is it for want of trust in Thy promises? Have we not cried day and night before Thee?' she added in a suppressed chant, clasping her hands.

As they looked, a little boat or canoe put forth from the opposite side of the stream, not the main flood of the Nile, but one of the branches that flow through the Delta. The first thing the two girls did was to hasten in different directions with their vessel of water to a low mud-built hovel, in front of which an older woman, with thickly-veiled head, was sitting shelling peas.

'Mother, Mirglip's boat is in sight. He is bringing home Dumah'; and not waiting for an answer, she put the water, brown and muddy-looking, but very sweet, down by her mother, and ran down exchanging the greeting, 'Peace be with you,' with the two men, or rather lads, in the boat, and holding out her hands to catch the rope by which it was to be hauled in. Both were handsome youths, the elder not more than eighteen, but sunburnt, and very scantily clad, the upper part of their bodies bare, and only a kilt reaching to the knee below, and much mud adhered to them.

'Have you brought more tidings?' asked the girl eagerly.

'Tidings indeed, Axa, said Mirglip; 'the saying is that we are to depart after another week.'

'Only another week of bondage! Oh! but we have hoped so often, and Pharaoh has always changed his mind!' sighed Axa.

'Even so,' said another voice, of a middle-aged man, who looked over the partition bank. 'What has Moses yet done for us save bring on us heavier toil and harsher treatment from our cruel masters? If his magic causes them to suffer, they do but revenge it upon us!'

'Shame, shame, Hatapha, to speak of the prophet as a magician. Thou knowest how the spells of Jannes and Jambres failed before him,' said Mirglip.

'And all he does is in the name of the Lord God,' added Dumah.

Hatapha made a kind of objecting sound.

'Besides,' added Mirglip, 'none of the miseries of Egypt have touched us. Neither the darkness, nor the hail, nor any of the strange troubles.'

'Oh! I doubt not that he favours us and would fain become our sheikh. What is his new device?'

'It is one in which we have our part,' said Mirglip. 'Elishama, the son of Ammihud, our Sheikh, bade me bear the message to us on this side of the stream, namely, the command which he heard from the lips of Aaron himself.   Each of us who is head of a household is to take a lamb, a perfect, unblemished lamb, and keep it separate from this night till the day of the full moon.   Then it is to be killed.'

'Killed!' exclaimed Hatapha.   'Does he want to bring the Egyptians down on us to make an end of us at once?'

'Perhaps it may be well that we should run some risk for the Lord's sake.   He who has done so much for us,' whispered Axa, who was standing beside Mirglip.

'A sacrifice, a sacrifice such as our fathers have told us of,' exclaimed Sherah, the mother of Axa; 'such as they used to offer to the Lord before our father Joseph brought us down hither.   Oh, blessed be the Lord God of Israel!'

'Methought sacrifice was put off till our long-talked-of journey into the wilderness,' still grumbled Hatapha, 'lest we should be

an abomination to the Mizraim.   Imagine the
men of Pharaoh seeing the smoke of these
offerings.   They would burn us on our own
altars.'

'These lambs are not to be burnt, good
Hatapha,' said Mirglip.   'They are to be
roasted whole with fire, and eaten by the
whole household together.   And listen,' as
Hatapha made a gesture of dislike, as of a
man always accustomed to a vegetable diet,
'the eating is not all.   The blood of the
lamb is to be caught in a basin, and the
master of the house is to take a bunch of
hyssop, dip it in the blood, and strike it on
the lintel and the two door-posts.'

'And for what strange purpose of Moses
and Aaron is this curious and unpleasant
ceremony intended?' asked Hatapha, with
his sneering look.

'No purpose of Moses, but the purpose
of Moses' God and ours,' returned Mirglip.
'The Lord, the Lord Jehovah, will visit the
land, and His angel will smite the first-born

in every house unmarked with the blood, but spare all those where the door is marked.'

'Only the first-born! What a well-informed angel he must be,' said Hatapha, turning away scornfully.

'But listen, listen,' entreated Sherah. 'If thou canst thus save thy child, wilt thou not?'

'I can save him better by husbanding my flocks and giving no offence to the masters,' said Hatapha. 'Pray, how is this to lead to our deliverance?'

'We are to eat the lamb at night, all prepared for travelling, for the Egyptians will turn on us in their grief and anger, all too eager to thrust us out, and so, by the death of the lambs, our freedom will be purchased!'

Hatapha turned away, as one resolved to hear no more, but Sherah remained in deep meditation. She was the grand-daughter of Beriah, the son born to Ephraim in his old age and bereavement. And she had heard from the old men, who had come out of Palestine in their boyhood, traditions of the lives of their fathers, and of the worship at the burial of Jacob. She knew, as did all the descendants of that great forefather, Joseph, that his remains, carefully embalmed and encased, were preserved in readiness to be carried back to the land of promise. The hope had ever been kept before her eyes. She was the only daughter of her family, her elder infant brothers had all perished under the cruel decree of Pharaoh, and her parents had removed to the farther side of the Delta, hoping to escape the watchfulness of the guards. Only a daughter had been born after their removal, and her husband, El-shah, was one who had been saved by the contrivance of a nurse. He had been a shepherd, and he was killed in resisting a foray of the Hittites on the desert side, leaving her with two infant children, Axa and Dumah. His brother Ulim had always been very good and helpful to her. He, too, was descended from Beriah, and thus was held as the head of his division of the tribe, which was called the Ben Beriah, or sons of Beriah. This, however, only caused him to be treated by the Egyptians as a foreman or taskmaster among the Israelites, and to receive a double quantity of punishment if they failed in their burthensome tasks. Their neighbour, Izhar, a Levite, had fairly broken down under the heavy exactions laid upon him, and had died soon after the calls of Moses began.

The works in which they were engaged were the potteries on the other side of the river, where very beautiful ornaments were made in red, black, blue, and white. Here toiled, among the sons of Shelah, of the tribe of Judah, young Dumah, son of El-shah, and likewise Ulim's three sons, Adoram, Mirglip, and Zemira, as well as Korah, the son of Izhar, and Hatapha, partly of Ephraimite, partly of Egyptian blood, who had married an Egyptian slave maiden.

More distinct instructions arrived on the following days, and it was decided, under the sanction of Elishama, the venerable Sheikh of the tribe of Ephraim, that Sherah's household, being very small, could join that of her brother-in-law Ulim in the midnight feast. Indeed it was she who furnished the lamb, not without tears on the part of Axa, for she had brought it up and petted it, as the child of one of the ewes that had escaped the Hittites. 'But,' said Sherah, 'it must be the whitest and most perfect. What God calls for must cost us something.'

Hatapha held apart, and only laughed when his wife Malbeth entreated him to conform to the ways of their neighbours for the sake of their children. He declared that it was too much to expect of him to give up any of his scanty flock for the sake of the magic rites that Moses pretended were inspired by his God, and even the authority of Elishama did not convince him, or change his determination.

Keren, the daughter of Izhar, on the contrary, went about singing and rejoicing so loudly that her stepmother, a feeble woman, feared that she would rouse the anger of the Egyptians, and she was obliged to pour forth her eager hopes as she sat in the door of Sherah's hovel spinning or embroidering with the women there.

Would that exquisite piece of work in wool really have to be given up to be worn by the Egyptian surveyor's proud thankless dame ?

Dumah and Mirglip, whenever they could get home, hung round the door, rejoicing in the sweet voices and hymns that began to be of hope instead of mourning.

CHAPTER II

THE PASCHAL MIDNIGHT

When the first-born of the foes
  Dead in the darkness lay ;
And the redeemed at midnight rose,
  And cast their bonds away ;
The orphaned realm threw wide her gates and told
Into freed Israel's lap her jewels and her gold.
                                        KEBLE.

THE night had come. The full moon was
shining, when, in the court of the house of
Ulim, there assembled himself, his wife
Zillah, his sons Adoram, Mirglip, and
Zemira, his two daughters, and likewise
Sherah, with her children Dumah and Axa.

They had entered, looking up at the lintel
and posts of the door, scored with a broad
mark of still dripping blood, one dash long-
ways, one crossways, and, contrary to their

usual habit, they stood round the table, where lay the lamb, whole and pierced with two wooden skewers, one the whole length of its body, the other across the shoulders. A large bowl of green herbs stood beside it, and a pile of flat cakes of unleavened bread. Ulim stood, and with clasped hands uttered a short prayer or grace, that the God of their fathers would accept the lamb they partook of in His name, and deliver His people from their sore bondage and captivity, and then all, solemnly and gravely, began to eat, using a knife to assist in pulling off the meat, but taking care not to break or divide the bones, flavouring with a little salt, and with alternate handfuls of the pungent herbs, and pieces of the thin cakes. No one durst speak at first, but when they had nearly finished, Ulim began to chant the lament of Heman—

'O Lord God of my salvation, I have cried day and night before Thee.
Let my prayer come before Thee : incline Thine ear unto my cry.'

Adoram, Mirglip, and Dumah began to make preparations for burning the remains of the lamb, according to the directions of Elishama, and the women were about to go out into the moonlight, when they became sensible that a strange dark oppression was over all around. They lost sight of the water that had glittered in the soft light, the stars that had shone so clearly had grown dim, their own dwelling could hardly be seen. They stood clasping one another's hands, and recollecting how there had been in other parts of Egypt the darkness that could be felt, when suddenly, just at the ' noon of night,' there came an awful rushing sound, as of a mighty wind ! They all fell on their faces and durst not look up till all was still ! When Axa did so it was bright silent moonlight again. The Southern Cross shone on her from the horizon, but at that moment, from Hatapha's house, there rose a fearful wailing cry. Sherah's first impulse was to spring up to hurry to her neighbour Mal-

c

beth, but as she gained her feet, an echo as it were of the cry burst out from the opposite bank, and in another minute there were shrieks ringing out from far and near. Both she and her sister-in-law turned, trembling and awe - stricken, to their own sons, but Adoram and Dumah were standing unhurt, as they had been when burning the lamb.

'The first-born!' said Ulim solemnly. 'God be thanked and praised!'

'Oh! poor Malbeth!' sighed Axa; 'but hark! Oh! that scream is from the surveyor's dwelling. His son, that proud fierce son, must be stricken!'

It was a place where there were chiefly Israelite abodes, so that the wailing cries came less thickly, and more distinctly; but from beyond, lower down the river, there was an ineffably awful sound swelling the air, one universal voice of horror and lamentation from thousands, absolutely thousands of voices, came rolling along with the stream, and though all the two households were untouched they were full of dread and dismay.

Sherah, as soon as she could move, still thought of the poor mother next door, but they heard her hotly wrangling with her husband, declaring that it was all his fault, and that he might have saved the child, while he made some contemptuous answer about not believing in superstitious enchantments.

Every now and then the lament seemed dying away, only to break out louder and wilder the next moment. Ulim began to bestir himself and to bid the young people assist him in bringing together their belongings, the few cattle that remained to them, the tent that Dumah's father had used, and the like, for he had fully accepted what Moses and Aaron had announced, that this night would bring deliverance. Just as morning dawn began, the hitherto proud and rude Egyptian wife of Amtou, the overseer of the district, rushed up to them.

She was a great lady, very rich and stately, but now her hair was flying wildly, her veil streaming back, her face torn by her nails. She carried a cloth in her hand, and dropped it before Sherah. 'Take, take it,' she cried, 'and begone! Begone in the name of your God, and let Him spare the others! Oh! my son, my first-born son of my hopes! son of my love!' and she hurried away, as fast as she had come, wringing her hands, and shrieking and sobbing in frantic grief. Again Sherah longed to say a word of comfort, but Zillah withheld her, and as they opened the cloth, bright gold ornaments were revealed, and Sherah and Axa well knew some of them, as the jewels that had been seized by Amtou to compensate for their tax, when they were left poor by the loss of their cattle and the father had been killed.

One was a beautiful fillet or coronal of lilies and filigree work containing turquoises, rubies, and lapis lazuli, which had come down from Asenath, the wife of Joseph, and another thick rough clumsy gold ring was said to have belonged to Rachel. Sherah had grieved much when they were taken from her, but at the moment she accepted them as another token of the fulfilment of the assurance that they should 'spoil the Egyptians' as part of the general restoration and triumph of their departure.

A boat was coming across the river. It brought a messenger from Elishama, their chief, to them and the other Israelites on their side of the stream, to be ready for instant departure, and desiring them to halt for the first time at the border of a wood to the eastward.

And already Egyptians, crazed with grief, were rising on the Israelites, some like the wife of Amtou, ready to pay them back all the past exactions, others fierce with revenge for the sufferings caused on their account, so that Ulim, though not apprehending actual danger, drew the Israelites around him for mutual protection. A surging sound, as of a great multitude, approached like a flood, and as the sun rose, as far as the eye could reach, was to be seen one moving mass of covered heads, interspersed with necks of camels, horned heads of oxen, and flocks of sheep, coming from all quarters, but chiefly from the rising city of Rameses, where most of the people had been employed on the bricks.

They came on, some bewildered and helpless, some chanting songs of deliverance, some anxious over their possessions. The little household of Ben Beriah were swept on with them as it were, exchanging with those who joined them histories of the awful night, how every Egyptian family was bewailing the sudden loss, except the few who had imitated the Israelites with the 'blood of the lamb,' how the palace of Pharaoh was full of grief and consternation over his cherished heir and the infant grandson, and even the captive at the millstones was bewailing her child.

The slaves of the priests at Memphis,
who attended the white bull Hapi (or Apis)
brought word that the whole college of
priests and virgins were frantic with grief
and despair, for their bull, whom they held
as the incarnation of the beneficent deity,
had perished by the same stroke as cut off
all the first-born of cattle. The priests
especially hardly regarded the death of their
own eldest sons in the desolation of the loss
of Apis, and likewise of the calf destined in
due time to succeed him, and their fury had
been such that the slaves felt that only the
protection of the Lord God could have
averted general slaughter.

When at last there was a halt, as twilight
came on, at the spot where Elishama had
previously advised Ulim to wait for him, it
was with gladness that Dumah pointed out a
canopy which he knew had been prepared to
be carried over the wrappings of the mummy-
case of Joseph. Elishama and his grandson
Oshea kept guard over the bearers. Oshea

was the hope and honour of the family since
his father Nun had died under the violence
of the Egyptians.   There was a pause at
this place.   It was beyond the most thickly
inhabited parts of Egypt, and some of the
wandering races of merchant Arabs, who
kept cattle, and brought articles of traffic,
haunted it.   The Israelites bivouacked for
the most part under a kind of shed made of
branches of the trees of the forest, a fact
commemorated in the name given to the
place—Succoth—and celebrated to this very
hour by the Feast of Tabernacles.

For indeed it was the first night that they
slept with the sense that bondage was over,
and no Egyptian whip awaited them.   Songs
of praise and thankfulness arose.   Sherah and
Keren led the way in turn in their own band
with the never-forgotten blessing of their forefather :

> Joseph is a fruitful bough,
> A fruitful bough by a well,
> Whose branches run over the wall.

The archers have sorely grieved him,
And shot at him, and hated him ;
But his bow abode in strength,
And the arms of his hands were made strong
By the hands of the mighty God of Jacob.

'Archers shot at him! Ah, well may you say so!' sighed Malbeth, breaking in on them, with her remaining babe in her arms. 'My boy, my first-born! We had to leave him, hastily thrown into a pit, poor child, for the savage Amtou was upon us, driving us away, though we had the same measure as himself—thanks to my husband. Pray our God to visit it on him! But wilt thou let the little one who is left sleep in thy tent, good Sherah? I fear the dews and the moonlight for him, under the boughs that are all we can get.'

'I believe our God will guard us from all baneful things,' said Sherah ; 'but if it will make thee more at ease I will take the little one in for the night.'

Hatapha was gone, as well as some of the other men, to endeavour to purchase tents

from the Arab tribe, and, perhaps providen-
tially, an extraordinary number of these
camels'-hair tents were on sale, or rather
exchange, so that after the first two nights
the Israelites, by various means, began to
obtain shelter, and the tribes in some degree
drew together under their respective sheikhs
or princes, always descended in direct line
from the original twelve patriarchs, and each
in immediate communication with Moses.

CHAPTER III

THE RED SEA

Soon shall a mightier flood thine arm
And outstretched rod obey,
From west to east the watery wall
From Israel shrinks away.

KEBLE.

'WHAT is this?' exclaimed Hatapha, as after a couple of days' journeying on the well-trodden track leading northwards to Palestine, the order was passed down to turn to the south-east.

'So far as I understand,' returned Mirglip, 'it is to avoid passing through the Philistine country.'

'Thou pretend to understand! Where is thy father?'

'He is gone to hold conference with

Elishama, through whom the orders came,' answered Mirglip.

'No one listens to me, or I could show you and them that this is marching right on the sea, whose waves are a good deal worse to deal with than the Philistines,' declared Hatapha.

'Without question, Moses knows where the sea is quite as well as thou dost,' replied Mirglip. 'But look there!'

'I see. I see a black-grey cloud hanging in front of us. If that be our front——'

'And,' said Mirglip, 'didst not see the same at night—not grey, but full of a calm, bright, shining light?'

'Malbeth said something of a light, but I thought it one of her imaginations.'

'Ah, knowest thou not,' said Mirglip, under his breath, 'that there the Lord makes Himself known to Moses? There is our Guide.'

'Hast not marked the inner brightness?' whispered Axa, with clasped hands.

'Oh! if meteors are to be our guide I have no more to say,' scoffed Hatapha.

'We shall soon be either in the sea or captured by the Mizraim, and sent off to labour in chains at the mines beyond Thebes —those that are not slain.'

'Children, children,' called Sherah, from the back of her ass, 'come hither. My saddle needs adjusting, Mirglip, and thou, Axa, thou shalt ride while I walk.'

They both perceived that it was to withdraw them from the faithless murmurs of Hatapha, and as Axa obeyed and rode along on the ass, it was with eyes anxiously bent on the shadowy pillar of cloud reaching from the skies, but to her fancy seeming to spread undefined wings hovering before the moving host, and reminding her, as rainbow brightness flickered on the borders, of the plumage of her own doves, which were carried in a wicker cage at the saddle. There was something in the sight that gave her a strange sense of soothing and protection.

By and by Ulim returned with tidings that added to Hatapha's discomfiture, except

that he could still say, 'I told you so.'
The Egyptians had rallied from their first
consternation ; and their thoughts were of
revenge and recovery of their slaves.   The
chariots of Pharaoh were being collected, the
troops marched up from Upper Egypt, and
without loss of time would fall upon the
fugitives.   Yet still Moses persevered in the
progress, over rough, broken, desert ground,
where the view in front disclosed the peculiar
reddish tint of the Gulf of Akaba, and beyond it the dark purple crags of the
mountains.

'Madness,' said Hatapha, and others besides Hatapha were staggered.   'Red! yes,
well it may be red!   It will be redder yet,
when we are mown down like sheep for the
slaughter.'

And when the sun was setting the multitude halted and looked back.   There was an
ominous flashing behind them, that they knew
too well to be the reflection from helmets
and shields of brass, and the bright harness

of war chariots. Each chariot, as the fugitives were aware, was drawn by two horses, and carried two warriors, one to drive and the other equipped with sword, and darts to be thrown.

Before them was the sea, rugged hills full of cliffs on the south and west ; behind them the enemy, roused to savage revenge. Even Dumah and Adoram trembled, and hoped to sell their lives dearly. Zillah wept, but Sherah prayed aloud, and Axa believed her when she said that God would never have brought them thus far to desert them now. Ulim and his sons had gone in search of Oshea to ask whether they should draw up in array round him in defence of the women. They found him attending on his grandfather, who was standing listening to the great Leader. Moses was standing on a small eminence, and the pillar of cloud hung over his head. His voice, as there he stood, rod in hand, overpowered the dull murmurs of the multitude, and penetrated far beyond his natural power, as he spoke—

'Fear ye not! Be still. Stand still, and
see the salvation of JEHOVAH, which He will
show to you to-day. For the Egyptians
whom ye have seen to-day, ye shall see
them again no more for ever!'

With this assurance Ulim returned to the
encampment of his wife and sister, and
Zillah's spirits revived, while Sherah smiled,
and said, 'I wait to see how the Lord will
save us!'

'And look, mother!' cried Axa. 'See
the pillar!'

The pillar had spread itself, as it were,
as twilight came on. There was a strong
east wind blowing, so strong that it knocked
down some of the shelters of branches, and
Mirglip and Adoram had to struggle to
fold up the tent. They had no darkness to
contend with. The cloud, whether from
reflected moonbeams, or from its own inher-
ent radiance, gave full and sufficient light;
and presently Zemira, whom Ulim had left
to receive orders, came running up.

'Are we to turn back to follow the cloud, and fight the enemy?' asked Adoram.

'No, no; we are to go forward. The cloud is as a curtain between us and our foes. It is light here, but one who looked beyond our camp says that on the north side all is one dense, confusing fog. He well-nigh lost himself in it, and the Egyptians are altogether bewildered, shouting to one another, and scarce daring to move a step.'

'And are we to go forward?' asked Ulim.

'Yea, Elishama and Joseph's bier are moving.'

'Into the sea?' cried Malbeth.

'As well be drowned as murdered,' said her husband. 'We cannot be left behind!'

The moving multitude in fact carried them on with it.

'We cannot fear with that marvellous light sheltering us,' said Sherah, looking up, as though she beheld more in that cloud than did the others.

'We are in the sea now,' whispered

Dumah, as he trod on a damp shiny piece of coral.

Axa touched him to make him look round to the westward.   The east wind was forcing back the waves.   They stood up, rearing one upon another, the white foam glancing in the strange light, while the strong rush of wind kept them back.   After Hatapha's first murmur of 'Moses knows the tides; he had best not trust them too far,' the Ben Beriah never spoke during the transit.   Some prayed, some looked to their steps over the rough shingle.   It was with morning dawn that the shoals stood up higher, the ground rose into a beach; and as they gained the shore and looked back, the wall of heaped-up waters became more visible.

'What of the enemy?' muttered Hatapha. 'Such a shallow gulf as this will be nothing to them.'

'They were lost in the fog, and fell into the mud and marsh,' said another Israelite. 'The chariots stuck fast there.'

'Ah, but with daylight—— Here they come!' exclaimed Hatapha. 'We shall barely have time to hide in yonder rocks.'

'Nay,' said Ulim. 'See, there is Moses on yonder rock. He holds out his rod! Stand still and see the salvation of God!'

The flood-tide had set in, the wind had gone down. The Egyptian chariots were in the bed of the sea. With a sudden roar and rush, as of an unchained wild beast, the imprisoned waves leapt down, and there was one minute of tossing, unbroken watery waste. Chariots, horsemen, horses, had vanished beneath it.

There was an awful pause. At first no one dared to speak. Then there broke out a wild shout of exultation from the mighty mass of men, as they felt they were safe, and that their enemies had perished, and as they saw one dead corpse after another floating up on the surface or cast upon the shore.

Some fell on their knees with uplifted hands towards the pillar of cloud; others,

probably by far the greater number, hurried
down to despoil the dead of their armour
and rich garments ; and the chiefs and elders
of the families felt bound to go and endeavour to prevent tumultuous quarrelling ; but
meantime a messenger from Miriam, the
sister of Moses, reached the women of Ben
Beriah, to call them to join in her thanksgiving. They gladly obeyed the summons,
and they found her standing on a slight elevation of ground, her thick veil hanging back
from her inspired face, her hands holding the
timbrels, and the women gathering round
her—foremost of them Keren, the sweet-
voiced daughter of Izhar. She struck the
timbrel and began the solemn dance, as they
sang in responsive strains—

Sing ye to the Lord.   He hath triumphed gloriously.
The horse and his rider hath he thrown into the sea !

CHAPTER IV

QUAILS

Sound the loud timbrel o'er Egypt's dark sea !
Jehovah hath triumphed—His people are free !
Sing—for the pride of the tyrant is broken,
    His chariots, his horsemen, all splendid and brave—
How vain was their boasting, the Lord hath but spoken,
And chariots and horsemen are sunk in the wave.

T. MOORE.

'A NEW, new life has begun!' cried Axa, as she came forth from the tent in the morning. 'A new life, delivered from all slavery and bondage.'

'Bound only to follow our beneficent protector Moses,' rejoined Mirglip.

'And in him, our God,' added Axa. 'See, the pillar is there, over the tents of the Levites.'

'What will be our journey? said Mirglip,

as he led up a goat for her to milk. 'That chain of red mountains looks very desolate.'

'Thou dost not fear?' exclaimed Axa.

'Fear! I fear nothing now I am free! but I wonder whither we shall be led.'

The hills before them, which bear the name of Attakah, meaning deliverance, were indeed of alarming aspect. Crimson and scarlet in the rising sun, and apparently devoid of any kind of vegetation. Around there were grass for the cattle, and a bush called camel-thorn, retem or broom, and a few clumps of palm-trees. The cattle could live, but the water was brackish, distasteful, and unwholesome. 'Oh for the waters of our river!' sighed Dumah, after trying the cup beside the tent, and throwing himself on the ground.

Axa brought him a little milk, in a horn cup—taken from her goat, which followed like a dog. He drained it; but moaned and said it only made him more thirsty.

'You will have worse to bear,' grimly said

Hatapha, 'if, as they say, Moses means to lead us beyond those mountains—that is if we be not wise enough to turn back.'

'To bondage!' cried Dumah. 'Never! I had rather die.'

'I feel as if we must and should live,' said Axa, looking upwards.

At that moment there was a shout of joy in the distance. 'Water! they must have found water!' exclaimed Dumah starting up.

'Or Moses has found some juggle to satisfy them,' muttered Hatapha.

Dumah set forth to inquire the cause of the cry of gladness which broke out again and again, but he presently met Mirglip and Adoram bearing between them a skin of water.

'Joy! joy!' exclaimed Mirglip. 'Praise be to our God! He hath revealed to Moses how to sweeten the waters. He hath cast into them the bark of a tree, and they are as fresh and sweet as ever was the best water of Father Nile.'

'Praise to our God!' echoed Sherah. 'He makes the bitter waters sweet. His wondrous wood in the water brings safety.'

Hatapha tasted, Malbeth brought her child to drink, and they could not deny that the water was good, but Hatapha still declared—

'Now, it is more than ever plain that Moses is a magician! I might throw a dozen bits of stick into a pool and it would be as foul as ever, but he has only to mumble something over it, and behold it is a cure or passes as such.'

'Mumble!' cried Mirglip indignantly; 'it is a prayer to the Lord God.'

'Let him call it so: I never denied that the God of Moses is a mightier power than Hapi, and maybe than Isis, who hath power over the waters. If her priests were here, they might make the trial.'

'Silence, blasphemer! beware lest thou bring down the wrath of the Lord upon our tents,' exclaimed Ulim.

Hatapha shrugged his shoulders and went

muttering away.   Malbeth lingered a little.
'My husband is hard of faith,' she said.
'Yet, Sherah, may it not be that as Thot hath
power in Memphis, and Anhuri in Thinis, so
may the Lord Jehovah have more power in
the wilderness than in Egypt, though even
there he hath conquered Hapi and slain him?'

'O Malbeth, slow of heart! wilt never
believe that there is only one Lord Jehovah,
Lord of heaven and earth?' cried Sherah.

'I will believe whatever will save my
child,' exclaimed poor Malbeth, who was
more Egyptian than Israelite. 'It is because
my husband only mocks that I have lost my
first-born. Tell me what to do, good Ulim,
dear Sherah, to keep evil from my babe, my
Enhat.'

'Pray to the Lord, and Him only,' said
Sherah. 'Thus will harm be turned away
from thee and thine.'

As Malbeth turned away they saw that
her infant was hung from head to foot with
Egyptians' charms and amulets, little figures

with heads of cats and jackals and the like.

'That should not be,' said Axa, severely. 'How can she hope that her prayers will be heard if she clings to all those idol abominations?'

'Poor woman!' said Sherah; 'she knows little and loves her child. May God be merciful to her, and look not on her misbelief!'

For a few days the march of the great caravan was fairly prosperous, never out of sight of the sea, and through a plain, with mountain-tops to be seen in the distance, but near at hand plenty of grass for the cattle, and overhead, date palms affording excellent food; but by and by they turned off into a dreary tract of chalk, bare, shut in with steep cliffs of white, and beyond these tall crags, some purple even to blackness, some of all tints of crimson and red, some green. It was a desolate contrast to the soft fertile banks of Egypt which they could still descry

beyond the narrow gulf. Moreover, the
supply of dourra that had been brought from
the former homes was running short, and in
the evening's halt sighs and murmurs were
beginning again, when the guiding cloud
began to flash with mysterious radiance such
as betokened a special manifestation, and
Ulim, going up with his sons to receive
directions, returned with an assurance that
their needs should be fully supplied.

'How can that be?' asked Hatapha,
gazing round. 'Are we to eat the caper
and the thorn like the cows and sheep?—
and even that will soon fail us.'

As he spoke, Mirglip uttered a cry of joy.
A round plump quail came fluttering up from
the sea, and fell exhausted at his feet.

'One quail! One man's scanty supper.'

'Ah! but look there.'

Over the Gulf of Akaba there was visible,
obscuring the sunset, something like a heavy
dark cloud, which before long resolved itself
into multitudinous winged bodies, flying low,

as though exhausted by the flight over the sea, and dropping one by one among the tents of the Israelites.'

'The quails on the move!' was the exclamation.

For it was known that every spring immense flights of quails migrated from the distant lands to the south in Africa and Arabia to nest farther north. Such a troop, in huge numbers, had been mercifully directed over the Red Sea, to fall exhausted and unable to escape 'round about the habitations' of the hungry fugitives, who throughout the evening and half the night were gathering them up, cooking them for present use, and splitting them open to be dried in the sun for further stores.

Ulim gave thanks for them, and his companions joined; but Hatapha, of course, said, 'So far so good, but quails do not come every day. How will it be in future?'

'O Hatapha,' cried Sherah, 'canst thou not trust the Lord who has brought us thus far?'

CHAPTER V

MANNA

Haste, or ere the third hour glowing,
  With its eager thirst prevail
O'er the moist pearls, now bestrowing
  Thymy slope and rushy vale.
    Dews celestial,
  Left when earthly dews exhale.
                    KEBLE.

MORNING had come, and the mist lifted up
from the valley, when Axa went out early to
fill her pitcher at the wells of Moses, and
stood at first wondering at the whitened look
of the grass, as though a hoar frost, little
known, though now and then occurring in
Lower Egypt, had remained more perma-
nently than usual; or as if a hailstorm was
lying there unmelted.

No! it was not hail. She bent and took

up one of the small round apparently con-
gealed drops before her.   It was solid.   She
tasted.   It was delicious in flavour, sweet
like honey.

Mirglip came out at the same moment.

'Oh! what is this?' cried Axa.

'Ah! this is the bread from heaven of
which Moses spake to us.   Father, see!' as
Ulim appeared.

'Peace be with us,' said he.   'Our God
has given it to us.   Gather it, my children,
and return thanks.'

By this time men, women, and children
were emerging from their tents.   Some
stood wondering; some threw themselves
upon the strange new white drops, swallow-
ing them eagerly; some swept them up into
their burnouses to secure as much as they
could, as soon as it proved good to eat.
Only a few followed Ulim's example and
stretched out their hands in thanksgiving.
Little Enhat, Malbeth's babe, screamed with
delight at the taste, and held out his arms

for more; and Hatapha said, 'Ay! good for children while it lasts. Methinks I have heard that juniper bushes bear the like.'

'This doth not lie only on the juniper bushes,' said Sherah. 'It is God's own gift, the bread from heaven.'

Every one was found to have enough for the day's consumption. Whether it was eaten raw, or baked, or boiled with milk, it was equally palatable. And all lay down to rest satisfied as to food, though Hatapha might be heard scolding his wife for her improvidence in pampering her child so much as to have left no provision for the next day. However, when morning came and Axa looked out, the same white pearls might be seen, bestrewing the ground all about the encampment, though just here there were fewer juniper trees, and more of the bare chalk cliff with only broom and caper bushes springing in the crevices. So it continued for six mornings, and then came a day when the manna, as the white beads were called, by the name of the exudation on the junipers, lay far more thickly than before, in such quantities that not only Malbeth but even Zillah began to talk of storing it against the time when they should be among the more barren rocks.

But on the next day Axa came running back in consternation: not a speck of manna was to be seen on the grass, or on any bush around.

'O mother, mother, it has failed! What shall we do? Why dost thou smile, mother? Hast thou any further trust?"

Sherah lifted up the cover of the large earthenware vessel where she kept the manna for daily use, and behold! there it lay, white and fresh as ever.

'How can this be? It would not last before,' said Dumah, putting in his hand and tasting one of the grains. 'It is quite good!'

'My son! hast thou not heard what our fathers have told us, how when this earth was made, God rested on the seventh day and hallowed it? Rest was kept by our fathers in the good land, but in our bondage we could only pass it over, and now, here again is God's Rest, and our provision.'

And in truth the manna was given in full profusion on the eighth day, reviving the spirits of the multitude as they were called upon to proceed through a winding desolate mountain pass, growing gradually upward, and closed in with immense, almost perpendicular walls of dark marble, upon which, high up, they could see carved out the only too familiar cartouches of the Egyptians, the hawk of Pharaoh, the jackal's head of Anubis.

'Ah, well may he be here, the usher of the dead!' sighed Hatapha, 'for what is this but the path of the grave! Full soon shall we and our flocks lie at the foot of these crags dead, and the Egyptian gods will rejoice over us.'

It was a most dismal place, and strange noises made it more terrible, and truly a howling wilderness. Ulim, who had once been sent to fetch home turquoises from the

E

mines, had heard the sounds before and
believed them to be sand slipping down on
the mountain sides, but the thunder rolls
were very awful to the unaccustomed ears,
and they were soon accompanied by a more
terrible sound still, echoing through the
narrow pass and reverberating from the
rocks — the angry murmurs of a multitude
thirsting and despairing ; for there were
many among them who knew but too well
that the region they were entering upon was
waterless. A few mountain streams might
come as torrents through the wadys, but the
spring was far advanced and the agony of
thirst would begin, nay, it had already begun
for those who had not filled their water-skins
at Elim, and the patient cattle were lying
about exhausted.

Suddenly there was a silence, and then
the yells of fury were changed into a joyous
acclamation, a shout of absolute ecstasy; and
as the women stood anxiously listening while
Sherah declared that their God had saved

them once more, Mirglip came bounding
up.

'Water! water!' he cried. 'Moses with
his rod hath struck the great rock, and from
it hath come a river of living water, pure
and bright and plentiful.'

'Glory to the God of Israel!' exclaimed
Sherah, falling on her knees with clasped
hands to give thanks before she would taste
the water that her son held to her lips.

The maidens, Axa and her cousins Neria
and Elmina, were full of anxiety to see this
living stream, and as Ulim was still there,
the two mothers allowed them to veil themselves, and go to the rock under the convoy
of the brothers. Ulim, with others of the
sheikhs, was engaged in superintending the
coming of the huge numbers, who either
needed water for themselves or for their
flocks, and who would have trodden and
crushed one another down if they had not
been heedfully kept in due order, marshalled
according to their tribes and families. Stand-

ing upon a rising ground, staff in hand, and chanting forth orders, Ulim shook his head as he saw the approach of his sons and daughters.

'Ah! women and maidens will be everywhere,' he said.

'Nay, father,' said Axa, for she always gave him that title, 'our mothers said we might come and see the wonderful works of God.'

'So be it then, only hinder not them who are in need of drink.   Take them up yonder rock, where they can see, and not be in the path.'

The rock was steep, but on the summit stood Keren, the daughter of Izhar, with two or three other maidens.   They had just paused in their song of

> Water out of the rock,
> Streams from the flinty rock—

and they renewed them in ecstasy, striking the timbrel as an accompaniment, as soon as they had made room for the new-comers.

Axa looked eagerly.   Above were the soft
prismatic blinding rays that made the pillar
of cloud, soft grey at a distance, but nearer
and more intently looked at, a mysterious
softened glory.   Below was the dark red of
the limestone rock, from a cleft of which
rushed in a cascade of white foam the water
—water not muddy like that of the Nile—but
as delicious to the taste, and cold as ice, as
well as pure and clear as crystal.

There was no abatement of it.   What fell
and escaped the eager lips of man and beast
was evidently making itself a course along
among the scattered stones and *débris* of the
road.   'Will it be with us?' exclaimed Neria.

'There can be no fear!' responded Axa.
'While God is with us, who can dread that
all our needs will not be supplied?'

Keren struck her timbrels together, and
burst out again into song.

And thus the maidens returned to Sherah
and Zillah at their tents, in exceeding joy
and sense of freedom and protection.

Indeed it so proved that the stream which flowed from the rock, in its meandering course towards the Red Sea, around the spurs of Mount Horeb, was never for many months more out of reach of the Israelites, who were never during the ensuing year reduced to drought or famine. And ever did Sherah lead her children to give thanks over their simple food as for special bounty sustaining them.

CHAPTER VI

THE BATTLE OF THE BANNER

On red Rephidim's battle plain
The banners sank and rose again.
The tumult of the wild affray
Rolled round to Horeb's mountain grey,
Rolled down to thirsty Meribah,
    As Israel's host swept past,
And Amalek's fierce battle-cry
    Came surging up the blast.
Above the strife, the leader hung
With hands upraised and suppliant tongue.
                    MRS. ALEXANDER.

AFTER marvelling at the gushing water from the rock, the Israelites were again called on to strike their tents and move forward.

This day's march was far from being as dreary as the preceding ones, for the winding wady suddenly opened into a lovely valley, grass clothing it, and groves of palms and tamarisks adorning the slopes. Walls of pink porphyry shut it in, the summits broken and diversified both in shape and colour, and gradually rising to a blue mountain peak far off. Herbs and flowers sprang out of the sides of the cliffs, and there was a clear running stream over the rose-coloured rocks, looking as if the water itself were pink.

The palms were exceedingly beautiful and luxuriant, not trimmed as in Egypt, but hanging their fan-like branches where nature led them, some bending over the stream, some forming long bowery arcades where the clusters of dates hung invitingly under the feathery branches.

Here, in the shade the Ben Beriah set up their tents, and lay resting on the grass, hoping that their halt in this pleasant vale might be long. Axa sat listening in delight to the lovely note of the bulbul which was altogether new to her.

' Is this what we shall hear in the land flowing with milk and honey ? ' she asked.

' It is a foretaste, my child,' said her mother.

WADY FEIRAN

They fell asleep, lulled by the rippling stream, but they were awakened in the night by cries of terror and howls of attack, but a good way from their tent. Dumah took his bow and went out in haste to learn the cause. He was joined at once by Mirglip. Ulim went in search of Elishama, leaving Adoram to guard the women.

'Was it the Egyptians?'

'No,' Adoram answered; 'my father says we are too far for their pursuit. It is more like to be one of the desert tribes who would envy us our spring of water from the rock.

It proved to be as Adoram had said. The attack had been made on the extreme rear of the Israelites, who had not yet defiled through the wady, or emerged into the Wady Feiran; but were still about the foot of the rock of Moses, pasturing their cattle. They were chiefly Danites, and with them were many Egyptians and runaway slaves who had joined themselves to the Israelites and

were not amenable to the discipline exercised
upon the tribes by their elders. On them
had descended a troop of wild horsemen with
long spears, and they had carried off some of
the cattle, and even were in the act of seizing
a woman and her children, when Ahiezer,
the sheikh of the Danites, a man of huge
strength, had come to the rescue and saved
the woman.

But Ahiezer had sent to Moses to inform
him that in the darkness a defiance had
been shouted in the name of the sheikhs of
Amalek, the owners of the desert. Those
who wanted to drink of the springs of the
Wady must reckon with Amalek. Pfui,
runaway leprous slaves of the Egyptians!
Let them beware of meddling with the
rights of the lords of the wilderness! The
spoil they had borne away from their masters
would soon belong to Amalek! The scream
of wrath and defiance, echoing from the rock
side, had even reached the tents of Ephraim,
and Dumah could well be believed when he

hastened back saying how terrible had been the sound.

'There will be an end of our journey,' said Hatapha. 'Those robbers will roll down stones from the heights upon us. We are caught in a basin here, like the fish in the ponds in Raamses, and shall meet our death! Those Amalekites may well call themselves lords of the desert! I have heard of them, prowling about and cutting off the parties of the turquoise-diggers.'

'So have I,' said Ulim, 'but they are no lords of the desert! The sons of Ishmael and the sons of Edom are that, but these Amalekites are robbers driven out by the King of Elam, who have ever lived by preying on all around.'

'Wolves of the desert,' said Sherah.

'Wolves who will soon be preying on our bones,' said Hatapha, 'unless our chiefs be wise enough to make a treaty with them. They might be bought off with half our cattle, but even then they would constantly harass us. I could hear them grin and laugh on the heights, like the hyena on the Nile bank.'

'But the Lord is mightier than they!' said Sherah.

There was watching and anxiety all the night, but in the morning all was beautiful and peaceful in the valley, and it was known that no attempt at terms with the Amalekites would be made, but that a battle was to be fought with them so as to secure Israel from further molestation by them.

Cowed by their long bondage, men of any kind of courage were not frequent among the Israelites, but there was a certain proportion who had served in the Egyptian armies, and these either volunteered or were selected for the battle, because they showed courage, or because they possessed arms, chiefly those of the drowned Egyptians picked up on the shore. Oshea, the grandson of Elishama, was chosen as leader because he had had some training as a soldier against those enemies of Egypt who dwelt about the cataracts.

All the day there was no attack, only the hyena laughter of the Amalekites was to be heard on the heights, and if a stray goat or sheep wandered beyond the folds, it never came home. It was plain that ruthless enemies were waiting on all sides, and moreover each tribe had a 'mixed multitude' attached to it who could not be depended upon not to betray them to the Amalekites and share the spoil with them. Ulim and the elder men were on the watch all day and night, the elders were in council, and Mirglip, Adoram, and Dumah were with Oshea, being practised in the use of weapons, and learning to respond to his calls. Even Hatapha, a sturdy strong man, had joined with them in training for defence. Axa and her cousins kept watch over the flocks that were carefully guarded within the enclosure that had been made with waggons, and stakes cut from the wood. One of her favourite kids, however, was lively. It skipped to the top of a waggon, and when she tried to entice it down with handfuls of grass, it only butted at her in play, then leapt down on the other side.

She called in vain, then ventured a few steps to drive it back, when suddenly she found her veil snatched, her waist seized by a great brown pair of hands; a grim, bearded face, with a shout of exultation, was upon her. She gave one despairing scream, before the veil was stuffed over her mouth and eyes, but at that instant there was a sudden relaxation; her captor fell, dragging her down with him, but holding her so fast in his convulsive grasp that his struggles only added to her agony and terror. She had, however, found her mouth and eyes free in another instant to see Mirglip rushing to disengage her and lift her up, breathlessly demanding whether she was unhurt, as he carried her back; only then daring to believe that the blood which spotted her veil was that of the Amalekite.

'My dove, my dear one,' he gasped out; 'I threw my dart, knowing that even if I missed the robber and slew thee, thou wouldst rather die thus than be borne away.'

'O Mirglip, Mirglip, thou didst wisely.'

She sat up under the palm tree, and he brought water from the spring in a wide leaf to restore her, and at the moment her mother and his father, startled by the cries of Neria and her sister, hurried up. Axa sprang to her mother's embrace, and to assure her that she was not hurt.

'Ah! child, child, never stray beyond the fold,' said Ulim, not unkindly; 'as thou dost not know whether the enemy will take thee unawares.'

'How near they must be,' sighed Neria, peering anxiously through the wood.

'No fear while safe within, under the shadow of the Cloud, my maiden,' said Sherah, who had her arm round her own child. 'Only let us look up and be thankful.'

But that experience was a terrible one,

and Axa trembled too much to stray out of
the immediate confines of the tents the rest
of that day.

And on the next, the dawn was made
terrible to the camp of Israel by the braying
of horns of all kinds and by the yells of
defiance of the Amalekites. They seemed
to have mustered all their clan, and were
barring the outlet of the wady to the north,
the route destined for the Israelites.

Oshea's band of warriors was drawn up in
front of the encampment—the Ephraimites
being the van of the host, and the long
company of the rest of the tribes lying in the
rear for the far distance. Far above, over a
tall peak of red rock, hung the pillar of Cloud,
and just below might be seen the figure of
the great leader Moses, with arms outstretched
in intensity of supplication.

'Oh! there, there is the banner of Israel
beneath which we fight,' cried Sherah. 'Go
in that strength, O my son Dumah!'

The tents of the family were shaded by

the trees, but Zemira, an active boy of twelve years, climbed up one of the peaks of rock, whence he could get into the top of a palm tree, and could shout to those below how the day was going. 'Now, now, Oshea and his men rush on! Ho! ho!' he shouted with them, 'I see the bullock of Ephraim! On, on! Push with horns! Darts are flying! Arrows! A cloud of them. I cannot see. Ha! Amalek is flying; down they go! On, on Oshea, through the pass! Is Mirglip there? I would I were. Hark, the enemy yell in confusion! Our shout resounds!' and the boy swelled it with all his force as the Israelites were pouring on them through the pass. It could be seen how, in intense relief, after his agony of prayer, Moses on the hill-top let his hands fall, to be clasped on his breast in thankfulness.

But what is this? The Israelites are flying, the Lion of the tribe of Judah is pressed back. They are giving way! A fresh clan of Amalekites must have come up! Oh!

F

woe, woe, the spoilers will be upon the camp, the men must have gone down. Alas for Dumah and Mirglip! Better the slavery of Egypt than to be the prey of the robber Amalekites! Moses' arms are raised again in the passionate pleading for his people!

Behold, the wolf of Benjamin was leading a troop of desperate men to the rescue. They turned back the fugitives, rushed on headlong, to where, on a mound, Oshea stood gathering together the Ephraimites round his gallant little band, of which Ben Beriah was the nucleus—Judah's Lion, borne by brave Caleb, came to the front again. The shouts become victorious, Amalek was driven back once more!

But all was not yet over, the battle had still to rage on, hour after hour, nay, day after day, as fresh hordes of the desert robbers hurried to the scene of encounter where they had expected an easy prey, but where brave resistance and well-organised attacks had filled them with vengeance.

Ever Moses prayed, with outstretched arms towards the Pillar of the Divine Presence, and when he grew weary, and could no longer sustain the effort, his brother Aaron and his brother-in-law Hur might be seen supporting those arms in his exhaustion, as 'all the day long' he stretched out his arms on behalf of his people.

Sherah and her daughter and all their fellow-women prayed too, joining in the chant of prayer led by Keren's sweet voice. The second day had come, and the fight had become too distant to hear it, only Adoram had been carried home hurt in the side by an Amalekite spear, and while his mother and sisters attended him, told that the Serpent of Dan had been seen in good time to secure the victory by coming up from the rear, and finally breaking the last stronghold of the enemy, driving the remnants of the desert hordes so far away that no further attack need be dreaded.

All was thanksgiving when the warriors

returned, flushed with success and bringing their spoil. Their loss had not been great, and except Adoram's wound, the Ben Beriah had not suffered.

The next day, the elders of the tribes were convoked, and each assisted in building up a rude stone altar on the spot where Moses had held up his hands so long in interceding prayer, towards the radiant pillar which had been in truth the banner of conquest to his people. And therefore they called the place Jehovah Nissi, the Lord the Banner!

CHAPTER VII

THE ELDERS

When Israel, of the Lord beloved,
  Out from the house of bondage came,
Her fathers' God before her moved
  An awful guide in smoke and flame :
By day, along the astonished lands
  The cloudy pillar glided slow ;
By night, Arabia's crimsoned sands
  Returned the fiery column's glow.
SCOTT.

THE battle had been fought in the passes adjacent to the valley of Rephaim, not in the beautiful wooded oasis itself, and thus there was no immediate necessity for moving on, nor did the Cloudy Pillar, which the Israelites had learnt to consider as their guide, begin to rise from above the rude stone altar of the Lord the Banner.

Indeed Oshea and the soldier Israelites

were making expeditions to hunt the brigand
race of Amalekites beyond the Gulf of
Akabah, and thus secure the further march
from fresh molestation by marauders hovering round to cut off the stragglers who met
with no mercy.   From one of these excur-
sions Mirglip came home triumphant, bringing with him a crescent of silver such as
were worn dangling from the camels' necks,
also a pair of gold bracelets, a burnouse
richly striped with red, black, and white, a
dagger with a chased hilt, and a long lance.
All this he had won in single combat with an
Amalekite, strong and wiry, whom he believed to be the same who had attempted to
carry off Axa.

He realised now that he was a full-grown
warrior, and she a maiden, and that they
could no longer be on the terms of child's
play ; but as he came into his mother's tent
and his sisters rejoiced over him, he turned
to Zillah and besought her, ' Mother, I pray
thee to take the bracelets, and give them to

Axa, daughter of Elshah, and entreat her mother, Sherah, to give me the maiden to wife, her whom I have loved since she was a babe.'

Marriages among kindred were encouraged, and Zillah embraced her son, and declared that she loved Axa as a daughter, and should rejoice to do as he wished; but not till she had consulted with his father. 'And where is my father?' cried Mirglip starting up.

'Thy father has been summoned with Elishama to the tent of Moses,' replied his mother. 'It is thought that it is to do honour to Jethro.'

'Jethro? I know not the name,' said Mirglip, as he found himself obliged to sit still on the ground and eat the cakes of manna that Neria brought him.

'Jethro is the great sheikh of the Midianites, to whom Moses fled out of Egypt. It was his daughter whom Moses married, and now that the Amalekite robbers are cleared

away, he has brought her and her two sons
to join Moses.'

'He came with such a train of camels,
and goats, and attendants, all in striped
mantles!' added Neria. 'Thou shouldst
have seen them, but they came while thou
wert gone.'

'Methought the Midianites were robbers,
such as the Amalekites.'

'Some may be such,' answered his mother;
'the tribe is widely spread, and broken into
many families. Some have wandered far to
the north and east, and allied themselves
with the Ishmaelites, and these often come
with merchandise to Egypt. They are all
in very deed children of Abraham our
father; and this same Jethro, to whom
Moses fled, is a great sheikh and also a
priest, living on the slopes of Mount Horeb,
much as did Abraham before him. He is a
great and holy man, and all the princes of
the tribes, with the heads of families, are
gone to Moses' tent to do him honour.'

So Mirglip had to control his impatience
and content himself with the admiration of
his brothers and sisters ; Adoram was nearly
recovered, but had not been allowed to go
out with him.   However, Neria had run to
Sherah's tent, and not only did Dumah come
forth to look, but Axa stood in its entrance,
her veil over her face.   For since the adven-
ture with the Amalekite, a temper of maidenly
coyness had come upon her, and her mother
had not needed to tell her that her days of
free sport with her cousins were over, since
they were not really her own brethren.   So
she only looked through her veil at the
noble young figure of the brave lad, leaning
on the spear he had taken, whose point
flashed in the evening sunshine.   But as he
made a step towards her, those words, ' My
dove, my dear one,' rang in her ears, brought
a glow on her cheeks, and made her shrink
back within the shelter of the curtain of her
tent.

When Ulim did come back, he was too

much preoccupied to have much attention
to spare either for his son's prowess or his
love affairs.   It seemed that the old sheikh,
accustomed to government, had been shocked
at the numerous trivial questions of which
Moses was the only arbitrator.   Was it for
him to decide whether a stray ass was the
property of Gadi or Assai, or whether
Jared had unrighteously beaten Nethaniah's
mischievous boy ?   Jethro had insisted that
Moses should establish what was in fact a
regular organisation, based on patriarchal
lines.   The tribes were already great genea-
logists, and there had always been a loose
patriarchal government among them ; but
subjection and slavery had caused it to be a
good deal dropped and forgotten, and in this
halt at Rephidim there was time and oppor-
tunity to set all in order.   Each tribe had
already a prince, the lineal descendant of
the son of Jacob, from whom the clan took
name.   These would be the chief leaders of
their tribe, and beneath them there would

be about seventy altogether of chiefs of
families. Thus Elishama was naturally
already head of the tribe of Ephraim, and
his grandson Oshea would follow him in
dignity, but Ulim was under them chief of
the Ben Beriah. The tribe of Ephraim was
not numerous, owing to the slaughter of the
elder sons of Ephraim by the men of Gath ;
but there were other houses belonging to it
which had their chiefs, and there were commands from Moses that the families should
draw together, and the march and encampment of each tribe be kept distinct, instead
of being mixed together, as had been the
case to a certain degree at first. Moreover,
that in any matter of strife the males of
the family should do their part, the elder
should be the first to judge, the first appeal
should be to the prince of the tribe, and the
final judgment, if needed, should come from
Moses himself.

To separate one tribe from another, and
make each family understand to whom to

resort for judgment, was the work which had
to be carried out by each prince of a tribe
through his subordinate elders (or sheikhs
to borrow the analogous Arab term), and
Elishama had entrusted this task, of course,
to Ulim and others of the representatives of
Ephraim. Though in the main the tribes
kept together, yet the outskirts intermingled,
and the separation and definition of bounds,
especially where families had intermingled,
and in the case of the 'mixed multitude'
from Egypt, was a troublesome affair, in-
volving many murmurs and some insub-
ordination.

Even Dumah murmured that the tents of
Izhar were to be removed to those of the
Kohathite Levites, for he had become intimate with Korah, the most able and brilliant
of all the youthful Levites, possessed of the
gift of poetry and music, as was likewise the
beautiful Keren, leader of the maidens of
Israel in their dances and sacred songs.
Dumah was urgent with his mother to go

and demand for him Keren of her parents,
so as to prevent this parting ; but Sherah
thought her son too young as yet, the whole
state of things too unsettled, and she did not
wholly like his marrying out of her own
tribe, even into that of Levi, and a relation
of Moses.

She would not have been sorry to separate
Dumah from the household of Izhar, which
was much given to criticising the elevation
of the sons of Amram to the general leadership, declaring, in the spirit of cousins, that
they had an equal right to be consulted, and
that if Moses had been specially distinguished, still Aaron was not his equal, and
they saw no reason for obeying the mandate.

However, Oshea came down, and so
spoke with Korah that he decided on removing and marching with the rest of Levi ;
but Keren threw herself into Axa's arms
and wept as if they were to be divided by
oceans. Korah exchanged sword and bow
with Dumah, and the two men promised one

another unending friendship and support, and Dumah showed more vexation towards his mother than he had even dared to do when she would not go and offer for Keren for him before the cloudy pillar rose, and they had to go on their way.

CHAPTER VIII

THE LAW

Around the trembling mountain's base
The prostrate people lay ;
A day of wrath and not of grace,
A dim and dreadful day.

                    KEBLE.

SEVEN weeks had nearly passed before, after
breaking up from Rephidim, the Israelites
emerged from a narrow valley into a wide
open plain, enclosed on all sides by black, red,
and yellow granite cliffs, and in front a mighty
mass of perpendicular rock, like a gigantic
altar, standing up before them, and beyond
it arose, towering into the sky, the mountain
peaks of Horeb.

On the mound before the great rock the
pillar of cloud halted, and orders came to

the people that they should here encamp,
and prepare themselves for that great revelation from the Lord in the wilderness, which
had been held out to them when in Egypt.

The plain below was wide and open, with
streams and wells of water within reach,
grass and verdure of trees, and was altogether a most suitable spot for an encampment.   Here the tribes were to set up their
tents, with the strange awful sense that
something great and unknown there was to
occur, something that made the elder people
recoil from the idea of taking advantage of
the repose to speak of marrying and giving
in marriage.

Then there came orders that the people
should wash their clothes and avoid all that
was connected with personal defilement, in
the course of the next day of preparation;
while—more mysterious still—fences were to
be set about the sacred mountain to prevent
children or animals from straying upon it.

'It is the Mount of God,' said Ulim, as,

standing with Sherah and Zillah, he watched his young men obeying this command.

'Is it not where Moses was feeding his flock when the Lord appeared to him in the burning bush, and sent him on his mission to deliver us?' said Sherah. 'No wonder he holds it as holy beyond all others.'

'And more than that,' said Ulim; 'as we, the elders, heard, the Lord Himself is about to be revealed again on yonder mountain and to give to us His law, by which to bind ourselves to be His own peculiar people, a kingdom of priests, an holy nation.'

'Well, well may we so be bound,' cried Sherah. 'Hath He not brought us out of bondage, and purchased us to Himself by the redemption out of Egypt?'

'So did we, the elders, all exclaim,' said Ulim. 'So did those of the people who could hear. May they hold fast to that to which they have pledged themselves.'

Morning came, and with it an awful

darkness and cloud over the Great Altar Mountain of Sinai, nay, not merely darkness, but as if those solid granite cliffs were on fire, with no earthly fire, but rising up to heaven in volumes of smoke, while lightnings, blue and forked, darted hither and thither, and loud peals of thunder reverberated through the desert heights, echoing back and back in the most awful manner; while a trumpet voice became louder and louder, and the very ground shook with an earthquake.

There was unspeakable terror. Every Israelite fell on his face in dread and dismay. Nothing could be more awful than the sight, the sound, the knowledge. Yet there was a difference in the kind of terror. Hatapha and his wife were absolutely stupefied. They pulled down the curtains of their tent round them and cowered under them, hiding their faces and crying out at every peal of thunder or earthquake shock.

On the other hand, not only Axa and

MOUNT SINAI

Dumah, but Zillah and her daughters
gathered round Sherah as if she could
protect them, for while they lay trembling
she rose on her knees with the words, 'It
is the Lord! the Lord God of Israel! He
hath saved! He will save!'

Ulim had gone with Elishama to Moses,
nearer to the terrible Mount, and they
returned with faces pale with awe, and limbs
quaking, to repeat the warning that no one
was to approach. Moses himself alone had
gone up that first hillock, and brought back
to them and the rest that command, to keep
back, since sin and corruption must be
consumed by the very presence of the Most
Holy Lord God.

After having given this message, so full
of fear and reverence, they returned to the
lower Mount, and the people stood, knelt,
or lay prostrate, while the thunders, lightnings, and earthquake, were more frightful
than ever. And then there was a long, dead
stillness—a silence to those trembling hearts

even more awful than the sounds that had preceded it, and those who durst look up saw in the midst of the fire a thick black darkness, but to Sherah, it was as if she saw dimly a rainbow light about that cloud and something flickering, now like an eagle's wings, now like a lion's face, now like guardian horns, but never for a moment so that the eye could be fixed on them; they changed and were so misty with intense light contrasting with the darkness. And out from all came the Voice, the Voice speaking in thunder yet in distinct words that thrilled through every ear and heart—

> I am JEHOVAH thy God.
> Thou shalt have none other god than Me.

And the others of those Ten Words that have been impressed on countless memories, if not on hearts, through all the ages that have since rolled by!

There was a drawing backwards as that Voice came forth, not exactly a rush, except in the very outmost parts of the throng, but the multitude, lying prostrate, were farther off from the skirts of the mountain than before, and their universal trembling made hushed sounds like the wind in a great forest. Only those who durst raise their eyes could see that one figure of Moses standing upright before the flame. An entreaty, by no one person put up but by all the people unanimously, came up to him through the circle of elders that the terrific, direct words of God might be addressed to him alone, for they could bear no more, they should die if they heard again that Voice from the cloud.

The answer, conveyed through the elders, was, 'Fear not, for God is come to prove you, and that His fear may be before your faces that ye sin not.'

When that message had gone forth, through the elders, there was a cessation of the lightnings and thunderings, though the cloud with the intensely dark centre still rested on the mountain, and into the black dense darkness Moses might be seen ascending the almost perpendicular rocks.

There was a pause and a stillness, while the people began to rest and recover from their awe and terror.   Ulim, greatly exhausted, was assisted back to his tent by his sons; his wife ministered to him, and Sherah knelt by him, while with folded hands he went over those great precepts, and dwelt on that which he had heard. Moses, he said, had gone up to learn the full terms of the covenant which God was about to make with His people, of which they had already heard the main eternal features.

'But, my father,' said Adoram, 'are these laws so unlike those that we have already learnt to follow, even among the Egyptians? I thought to hear in that terrific Voice something closer and nearer, but except that regarding the Sabbath, and the last of all, they are only what every good man kept in obedience out of the honesty and uprightness of his heart. Without those rules, save what relate to our God Himself, even an Egyptian would not be admitted to the Hall of Osiris.'

'It is true, my son. It is the natural law within all human hearts, but I doubt me whether that makes it easier to be kept without transgression.'

'Nor have we heard all,' said Sherah. 'If I understand right, Moses is gone to receive further commands.'

'And we are to seal our covenant with God,' said Ulim; 'that covenant which, if we keep, will give us the possession of the land of our fathers, so long promised to Abraham.'

'These were the promises to our father Abraham and his children on condition that they believed,' said Adoram. 'We have believed. This is a new condition.'

'The promise to Abraham,' said Ulim, 'was that in his seed all nations should be blessed, also that his sons should inherit the land. Now we are to engage to keep that law which we have heard and our God will give us the land.'

'The land of milk and honey,' said Sherah, 'the land of olives and vineyards, of fair valleys of wheat and barley, the land where are our fathers' tombs, the land of rest. Oh! our God is good to us, and well may He call on us to serve Him.'

When Moses returned to the camp and summoned the elders, they brought back the outline of the judgments that the people were to observe, if they meant to devote themselves to their One true and awful God who had revealed Himself upon the mountain - top, with the assurance that His Angel should go before them, as in the Pillar, to bring them into the Promised Land. The Angel, the Messenger of the Covenant, was felt by the thoughtful to imply some most especial holy Presence, and they lived in a kind of trance of awe and expectation. Sherah, as in a blessed presence which enchained her thoughts and aspirations, Hatapha with a

sense of fear and impatience, forced to
believe and accept what he saw and heard,
yet wishing it was all over and he was free
to be himself again. The younger people
partook more or less of both feelings—Axa
and Mirglip feeling the most with Sherah,
Zillah and her other children more with
Hatapha, while poor Malbeth, bewildered
with terror, and thinking only how to save
her child, had torn off all his amulets and
charms lest they should offend Him who
spake from that dreadful darkness, and then
came creeping up to consult Sherah whether
she might not put them on again to defend
him against the spirits of the wilderness.

In early morning there was a summons to
Ulim, and by and by it was understood that
the children of Israel were to be sworn in to
the Covenant with the Lord God Jehovah,
with the same rites wherewith bonds and
treaties were made on earth between nations
and individuals.

The men were drawn up according to

their tribes, clans, and families on the plain.
The women stood by the tents, afar off.   But
Sherah and her daughters could see that on
the hillock beneath the lofty precipitous altar
mountain, which still was covered with the
cloud and fire, were raised twelve pillars, or
rather piles of stones, and in the midst of
them was an altar of stones, with fire burning
on it.   On that altar, Oshea, Caleb, and the
other young men of the princely houses of the
tribes, were with the sons of Aaron, killing
oxen and offering them up on the altar.   It
was an unaccustomed sight, for sacrifice made
no part of the Egyptian ritual, and had
been necessarily disused among the Israelites
during their time of bondage.   Axa and Neria
hid their eyes, shocked, though they were not
near enough to see the sufferings of the beasts.

'Nay, children,' said Sherah.   'See ye
not these poor animals are an atonement, not
sufficient, but an emblem of what we guilty
ones ought to suffer before we dare to come
before the presence of the Holy One?'

'But an ox is not worth the soul even of a little babe,' said Axa.

'No, indeed, child, but the shedding of the blood of the ox betokens that our shortcomings are laid upon One who is to come. May it be this Messenger who is to be with us.'

The offering completed, Moses, through the princes, rehearsed to each tribe the Ten Words, and likewise the other judgments which had been written down as they were spoken to him, demanding whether the people accepted them, and bound themselves to the covenant with God, engaging to keep the Law strictly, while He gave them the land of their fathers.

A shout as of thunder went up from hundreds of thousands of voices.

'All that the Lord hath said will we do, and be obedient!'

Then Moses took scarlet wool, and bunches of hyssop, saying, ' Behold the blood of the covenant which the Lord hath made with you concerning these words '—and all the tribes were sprinkled with the blood of the sacrifices which had been caught in the basons—the written papyrus also touched with the blood.   It was the solemn ceremony that pledged parties to a treaty, and there remained the eating of the animal sacrifices, as ratifying the agreement.

For this, the seventy elders, Aaron and his elder son, accompanied Moses higher upon the mountain.   Of the Presence that they saw there, when they did eat and drink, Ulim never could speak.   Awful and glorious, pure and clear beyond all power of description, or even of thought, it had been, and he could only remain transfixed as it were with the recollection of what he had been admitted to perceive.

CHAPTER IX

THE LIKENESS OF A CALF THAT EATETH HAY

If Aaron's hand unshrinking mould
An idol form of earthly gold.
KEBLE.

MOSES was on the mountain, within the thick dark solemn cloud, and his only attendant, Oshea, Elishama's grandson, had disappeared with him. That was all that was known to the camp of Israel, except that the great cloud still enwrapped the altar-like heights of Sinai, black with the darkness more than night in the centre, yet lighter on the borders, and at times flashing out with lightning flames.

Indeed, to some eyes it wore a different aspect from the appearance to others. Hatapha and Malbeth only saw the blackness and

fiery brightness, while Sherah almost always
beheld the flickering rainbow and hovering
shape of wings, and Ulim, Axa, Mirglip, and
Dumah saw it thus, not constantly, nor so
evidently, but now and then as they prayed.
Thus, more or less, it was with the other
families and households of Israel; some looked
above the mountain and were cheered, some
looked below and were terrified.

Keren, as Dumah reported, was in an
ecstasy of song, looking up to the mountain,
and now trembling at the manifestation, now
glorying in the great God, His victory over
idols, and the purity of His law.

Dumah longed more and more to bring
such an inspired being home to his tent, but
his mother continued to declare that this was
no time for marrying and giving in marriage,
and that a dutiful Israelite could only wait for
the present till the will of the Lord should be
more fully made known.

Moses was expected to return in a week at
latest, but the days were counted out and

nothing was seen or heard of him. Another week passed with no event; neither he nor Oshea could be heard of, and there began to be great anxiety.

'Of course they are lost,' said Hatapha; 'it was mere madness to ascend those cliffs, and especially in such a storm. They are no mountaineers! What could befall but that they should have been dashed to pieces long ago?'

'Besides, what could they find to live on,' added Malbeth, 'up on those bare peaks?'

'He who sends manna can nourish them,' said Sherah.

'Old Elishama seems wonderfully content, but I am sorry for poor young Oshea, his heir, and a youth of promise,' added Malbeth.

'It has all ended as I expected from the first,' said Hatapha. 'Moses has gone a little beyond his own magic powers, and has perished on the mountain, and now there is nothing left for us but to become desert wanderers like the Midianites, or to make the best of our way back to Egypt.'

Such sighs as these grew stronger every day, and after about three weeks had passed, Ulim came back to the tents of his family with the news that a deputation had come to Aaron from a large number of the tribes, declaring that it was vain to wait any longer for Moses, and that they must and would take measures for leaving the valley, and the neighbourhood of the terrible cloud, which had evidently engulphed their leader.

' And what said Aaron ?'

' He wavered.   He does not himself believe that Moses will not return, but he dreads the people's rage, and wishes to do something to satisfy and occupy them.'

'That is lack of faith and patience,' said Sherah.   'Who can fear while the manna daily falls ?'

But the next day a party of men came round, grave bearded elders for the most part, demanding of the women gifts of their earrings. It was understood that they meant to induce Aaron to try a kind of experiment or divination. Ulim, who had gone with Elishama to the leaders' tents in hopes of strengthening his hands, came back reporting that he was staunch in his trust personally, but that Nadab and Abihu, his sons, had persuaded him that this collection would occupy the disaffected, and keep them quiet till Moses returned. Of course none of the women of the Ben Beriah would contribute except poor Malbeth, who always did anything that she fancied might tend to the safety of her darling, and who presented them with a golden bead, fashioned with the jackal's head of Anubis, the supposed conductor of souls to their trial. It might bring ill-luck to the babe!

The faithful eyes among the Ben Beriah looked and looked at the cloud in the mountain, but all was still; there was no change in the appearance, and murmurs went about that merchantmen had spoken of mountains

II

perpetually burning, so that this might be a natural wonder, of which Moses, a learned man, had taken advantage. But the Voice and the Ten Words?

'I believe,' said Hatapha, 'that the magicians of Egypt could have made their oracles speak as distinctly.'

'Blaspheme not,' said Ulim severely. 'Or I shall cast thee from our tents.'

Ulim spake boldly, but the trial of patience was a terrible one, and he was only supported under it by the firm trust of Sherah, who held that God was trying them, and that they had need to be patient. But it was a sore and terrible trial when, on an ensuing day, it was known that Aaron had yielded to the clamours of the tribes, and allowed the accumulated gold to be cast into a disused furnace of the Egyptian miners.

That evening Dumah brought a veiled maiden to his mother's tent. 'It is Keren,' he said; 'Keren, the daughter of Izhar, my mountain roe, my gazelle, my dear one.'

'Ah, Dumah! ah, Keren!' she said; 'dost thou come with thy parent's consent? Remember the words we heard.'

'I remember them!' said Keren, throwing back her veil. 'I come with the consent and blessing of my father's wife and my brother Korah. He will not see the sons of Amram thus dishonour the God of their fathers, and hath sent me away ere there be heathen doings and a blood-stained vengeance. I would have stood and testified against them, but my mother and brother feared for me, and sent me away with Dumah. Woe to idols! Is Aaron's rod vain without the Lord?'

Keren's dark eyes and glowing face were beautiful with the fire of excitement, as she stood with head uplifted. Hers was a very different beauty from the gentle face of Axa, whose sweet brown eyes and tender smile told of love and humility.

Sherah was a good deal distressed. True, the father Izhar was dead in Egypt, and that his widow was not the mother of Korah,

whose young wife was at the head of the
tents of Korah.   She could not, however,
refuse to Keren the shelter of her tent, and
led her to her own inner apartment, to wait
till Elishama could be consulted.   The tidings respecting Aaron likewise filled her
with anxiety and grief that he should thus
far have yielded to popular clamour.

The next day Hatapha sought her laugh-
ing.

'What thinkest thou, Sherah?' he said,
'Aaron's plan for contenting the fools of the
congregation has resulted in?   None other
than that the melted earrings and the like
have run together into a misshapen lump
that the wiseacres of Israel declare to be
an exact likeness of our old friend Hapi.'

'It was the influence of the divine amulets and charms,' said Malbeth.   'There
were many teraphim there — Anubis and
Pasht and the rest.'

'The influence of evil spirits then,' said
Sherah.

'The influence of the fire!' said Hatapha, sneering as much at the dismay of some of the women as at the satisfaction of the others in what he not unreasonably viewed as a by no means extraordinary event. 'The gold had melted into such a mass as I have seen brought to be stored in Pharaoh's treasure house, but the eyes of the tribes see in it Hapi himself manifested, in the stead of Moses, to lead them.'

'Hapi! In the very face of those Ten Words?'

'Oh! the cry is that they do not deny that Jehovah is their God, but they need some visible manifestation to go before them as did Moses. And now that this is granted them they will follow it.'

'And what saith my brother? saith Korah?' cried Keren, breaking forth from the partition.

'Thou here, little prophetess?' exclaimed Hatapha. 'Oh, Korah? Oh, he and some of the more fervent Levites—Aaron's younger sons among them—have retired, sharpening their swords, I trow, in case there be any outbreak.'

'I knew it!' exclaimed Keren. 'They will stand for the honour of their God.'

In much anxiety did the Ben Beriah watch. Ulim had come home, disappointed and disgusted with the cowardice of Aaron, whose fears were inducing him to add with a graving tool a few touches to increase the likeness to a calf or ox in the mass which had at first appeared merely clumsy and shapeless; but the people were so determined to accept it as the emblem of their leader that he temporised and followed their bidding in fashioning the soft metal into something more like a calf, the only condition, as it seemed, of them accepting Aaron as their ruler since his brother had disappeared.

A feast of Jehovah had been proclaimed for the ensuing day, for the Israelites did not believe themselves to be forsaking the God of Abraham, Isaac, and Jacob. The Cove-

nant, so solemnly sworn to, and the Ten
Words from the deep dark cloud, or, as
Hatapha, who contrived to laugh at all, said,
some declared that the figure having come
out spontaneously could not be said to be
made with hands, nor did they mean to pray
to it as a god, only to use it as a symbol to
lead the way.   And Hatapha observed that
after all it was like really nothing in heaven
or earth.

The proclamation of the feast was heard
by the Ben Beriah with intense anxiety and
grief.   Elishama prohibited all the tribe of
Ephraim from taking any part in it, and
bade them rather mourn for the sin of their
brethren ; and all the more duteous ones
covered their heads, cast dust upon them,
and knelt in prayer that wrath might be
averted.   Keren could hardly be prevented
from rushing back to shriek forth her indignation,. and hurry on the vengeance of
her brothers, but Ulim and Dumah withheld
her, by all the love which was growing within

her for him, and by her parent's command, aware that so young a maiden would have little effect on the people, and might only bring danger on her brothers before the time for resistance.

But it was misery and humiliation to hear the shouts and cries of the exultant Israelites and the cadence of wild songs connected with the idol revelries of Egypt, and to remember therewith how lately the actual Divine Voice had spoken, and all had bound themselves to obey!

CHAPTER X

THE MEDIATION

But lest he should his own forget
Who in the vale were struggling yet,
    A sadder vision came
Announcing all that guilty deed
Of idol rite, that in her need
He for the Church might intercede
    And stay Heaven's rising flame.
               J. H. NEWMAN.

WHILE mad sounds of revelry were coming up from the camp, and making the faithful of the Ben Beriah weep over the sin of Israel, Axa lifted up her eyes to the mountain-top, now glowing with intense red light, and standing clearly defined in front of it were two figures, one bearing something heavy in his arms.

With a cry of gladness she declared,

'Moses, Moses! He is coming, and Oshea with him.'

'Coming, coming!' burst out Keren. 'Now will there be vengeance on all who bow down to gods of gold. Now will their joy become wailing.'

'They are pausing on the mountain path,' said Dumah. 'No doubt that foul outcry and riot have reached them.'

'There! What has he done?' exclaimed Axa. 'He has thrown down the blocks that he bore into the clefts of the rocks. Swiftly he comes—oh, how swiftly!'

'The angel of wrath must be speeding his path,' was Keren's exclamation.

Soon Moses was lost sight of, but Elishama and Ulim set forth to meet him, and very soon the shouts of revelry died away, and were succeeded by a stillness equally terrible, and presently after came shrieks and screams borne upon the wind. Malbeth, as usual in a wild fit of terror hid herself and her child in the tent, imploring the other women not to make it known that she had contributed any gold to the calf.

It was long before Ulim and his sons returned, and then they came with every sign of mourning. All, even the most innocent, were to put on sackcloth, and mourn for the grievous sin that had been committed in the camp. As to the chief of the transgressors, those who had driven Aaron on to the misdeed, and forced his hand, and who were performing a wild heathen dance round their idol, Moses had sent the more faithful Levites in upon them to execute vengeance upon them at once for breaking the covenant they had so solemnly sworn to. Korah and the other Kohathites had rushed in and performed the terrible edict that cut them off. Keren clapped her hands for joy, and was exultant that Dumah had gone with them.

By and by Dumah came back, his sword still showing the dire work in which he had been engaged. Malbeth, who had begun to

look out, shrieked and hid herself, as if she
expected the execution to fall on her, but
Keren flew out to meet him, and threw herself into his arms, glorying in his having
been among the avengers of the Lord's
honour; but his looks were pale with awe
at the terrible task in which he had been
engaged, and in which Korah and the other
Levites had been foremost. 'Were Aaron
and his sons among them?' was Keren's
next question.

'Nay, Aaron threw himself on his face in
deep repentance, and Moses promised to
intercede for him.'

'Ah! Moses ever favours his brother!
But the sons of Aaron?   Light-minded
young men, unworthy of the vision of the
covenant,' said Keren.

'Nadab and Abihu followed their father.
The younger sons, Eleazar and Ithamar, kept
close to their tent.   Methinks Elisheba their
mother hath more power over them than over
their elders.'

'She is a good and holy woman,' said Sherah, 'one who ever kept herself apart as much as might be from traffic with Egyptians.'

Malbeth here ventured to emerge from her tent with anxious inquiries for her husband.

Dumah had not seen him, and did not believe him to be in danger. He was far too wary and cautious a man to expose himself by the adoration of an idol which he despised. The execution, it seemed, had chiefly fallen upon some of the ruder and more disaffected of the tribes—Simeon, Gad, and scattered fragments of the other tribes who had lived much intermingled with the Egyptians and imbibed much of their idolatry. Even as Dumah spoke, Hatapha was among the family. Malbeth threw herself upon him in great joy.

'Foolish woman,' he said, putting her aside, 'didst thou fear for me? As though I had not wit enough to keep out of the follies up there. As though the Hapi, living and breathing, were not a ridiculous emblem enough for the God of nature that they should be content with a hideous cold lump of gold in his stead, or the stead of Moses, who, if he be a magician, is also a great and wise man, the only one capable of leading these thousands of senseless, stiff-necked people out of slavery into some sort of freedom, whether it be like the Midianites of the desert, or the much-talked-of Canaan.'

So poor loving Malbeth was able to tend her husband, while Sherah and Axa were glad to escape from the faithless tongue that always grieved them.

With the morning, there was silence and anxious expectation. The manna was found on the grass, and thence it might be understood that God had not forsaken Israel utterly; but a rumour went forth that He had made known that the actual Presence in the pillar of cloud should no longer be with them, just as those blocks or tables of the Ten Words, written by God Himself,

had been destroyed because of the immediate
infraction of them. Though all had not
partaken of the calf-worship, very few could
acquit themselves of impatient despair at the
long absence of Moses.

And the order came forth that all should
put away their ornaments from them, and
pray and fast, while Moses entreated for their
pardon. His own tent had been removed
to the mound, and Elishama believed that
it was by the Lord's command, that he
might be separate from the people when
wrath fell on them. Was such wrath to fall
on them? Even those who had stood aloof
from the 'similitude of a calf that eateth
hay' trembled, as conscious of many a
wrong. Keren might be joyous and
triumphant, secure that the Lord would
spare His own, but Sherah was full of the
recollection of many a past rebellious thought
or impatient word, and would not have
thought a sudden visitation of divine punishment more than her due. In sackcloth and

dust they waited, but at last, with joy and relief, the cloudy pillar was seen to be upon Moses' tent of meeting as of old, but cloud alone, not luminous, even to Sherah's eyes. The whole mighty host bowed down in one fervour of hopeful supplication, as they beheld the token of their pardon, of which Moses came and assured them ; but Oshea remained in the tent—Oshea, who had been the attendant of Moses on the mountain, had waited all those days, a resolute, patient sentinel outside the fiery cloud, and had descended with him to behold the disgrace and shame of the calf-worshippers, fancying at first that the tumultuous shouts of their orgies were 'a sound of war in the camp.'

He had been nearer to the immediate Presence than any man except Moses, and he lay prostrate before the pillar, at the door of Moses' tent, while the tidings of hope were spread abroad, yet still it was that an angel would guide them, not the Lord Himself, as hitherto.

There was long stillness, and at last, to Sherah's earnest eyes, the rainbow colours once more glimmered. She was sure that there was hope of restoration; and as evening fell, the light grew brighter. Ulim came to her tent, and said, 'My sister, come with me to Elishama's tent. Thou, who hast such strong faith, shouldest be there to hear what young Oshea has to tell.'

'Is Oshea returned?'

'Yea; Moses is gone up alone upon the Mount, and hath sent him back again. No doubt God hath some great work in store for him, for henceforth we are to call him Jah-Oshea.'[1]

'JEHOVAH the Saviour,' repeated Sherah. 'He only waited patiently in the dark cloud, while beneath, we strove, we fretted, and we sinned! Well may he be singled out as a leader to the Lord's salvation.'

'I believe it,' said Ulim; 'his face is not

---

[1] When Joshua received the name is not clear. It is mentioned in Numbers xi., but he is called so before.

I

as it was before! It is steadfast and yet glowing.'

So Sherah felt. There was a strange grave beauty and yet ardour upon the countenance of the young man, as he bent his head before her, in reverence to one who was a mother in Israel, and after leading her to a cushion beside his grandfather, he took his own place respectfully as ever before the elders, although he had been so high, and so near the Holiest.

He told, what drew Moses all the closer to their hearts, how the great leader had actually offered himself to God instead of his people, entreating, in his anguish of supplication, even to be blotted out of the Book of Life, rather than that they should not find mercy.

But even Moses was not worthy, nor sinless enough, to be accepted as an atonement. The answer came back, 'Him that hath sinned, him will I blot out of My Book.'

'Ah!' mused Sherah, 'not even Moses could be accepted in the stead of the people. No man may deliver his brother nor make agreement to God for him;[1] for it cost more to redeem their souls, so he must let that alone for ever. There is a worthy Lamb yet to come.'

Yet that intercession had availed so far that the covenant, though so flagrantly broken, was to stand, and the Israelites to go on their way to the Land.

Of that most awful and mysterious meeting that followed, Joshua would not, or durst not, speak, when Moses aspired to behold the very glory of the Lord, and because of the weakness of mortal flesh was only allowed to behold the after shine of His full Majesty and Brightness from the hollow of the rock, and to hear the proclamation of His Eternal Mercy and long-suffering.

Joshua only knew that the Presence in the Pillar was not to be withdrawn, and he

---

[1] The 49th Psalm is very early, of uncertain date.

had aided Moses in the hewing out of two
blocks or tablets to be carried up the mountain in place of the former ones, to be inscribed by God Himself with the eternal
law.

CHAPTER XI

The pageant of a kingdom vast,
And things unutterable, past
  Before the Prophet's eye.
Dread shadows of the eternal Throne,
The fount of Life and Altar Stone,
Pavement, and those that tread thereon,
  And those who worship nigh.
                    J. H. NEWMAN.

MOSES was another forty days out of sight on the mountain, but the people remained in quiet on the plain. Of course they had not the same fears for him as at first, and they were besides greatly humbled and subdued.

The worst, most lawless and most inclined to Egyptian idolatries, had been slain, and the foul revelry had left disease among many of the families who had participated in it.

Aaron too spent his time in constant humiliation and prayer in the tent of Moses, and
would fain have kept his two sons Nadab
and Abihu doing the same, but there was a
certain levity about them that seemed in-
capable of perceiving the extent of the
offence. They had never believed the calf
to be more than a lump of metal ; they had
only let the foolish people have their will.
When these had met their deserts, why
should they mourn ?

Keren, like her brother, found fault with
them, and declared that their apparent
humiliation, like that of their father, was
only to win favour with Moses and secure
the priesthood to themselves ; but she, together with all in Sherah's tent, continued
in a state of mourning for the general sin,
and put on no ornaments.

It was understood that Moses had received a great revelation as to the future
worship, and likewise more detailed teachings
as to the institutions of the Israelite people,

on his first stay upon the mountain, and that he was now being admitted to further instruction in some wonderful manner which would be communicated to them on his return.

And, looking for his return, they waited. Rain enough came to nourish grass sufficient for food for the cattle; the manna never ceased; and the robber tribes had been so effectually driven back that the camp was entirely unmolested by them or by the Egyptians in the rear, who were, indeed, in a state of confusion and disorder during the few remaining years of the Pharaoh Menephtah —after his losses in the Red Sea.

And during this time was carried out the exact numbering or census of the people, dividing each tribe by clans and families, classed by thousands, hundreds, fifties, and tens, according to Jethro's advice, which could be here more fully carried out than before.

Moreover, according to the commandment already delivered to Moses, each man above twenty years old was to offer the weight of half a shekel in silver (value about 1s. 3d. of our money) to be used in the service of the sanctuary about to be made; and it was added that pestilence would be the penalty of neglecting this ransom for the future in any census.

Dumah, Mirglip, and Zemira fell below the age at which this ransom was required, but Ulim willingly paid it and so did Adoram. 'Their redemption money,' Ulim said to Hatapha, who as usual grumbled, 'well may we give it to the Lord, who hath brought us out of our bitter bondage.'

'For that matter,' said Hatapha, 'we were told that our redemption was free! Half a shekel is a good deal less than an Egyptian would take for one of us.'

'True, but it is a token of what we owe to our God. A token—nothing like the whole.'

'Oh!' sneered Hatapha, 'and pray is that why, on such a penalty, it is to be continued to future generations?   A very convenient law for the priests that are to be.'

'Silence, Hatapha!   Thou goest near to blaspheming the ordinance of God!' said Ulim, with all the authority of a sheikh.

'God's ordinances reach on and have a meaning far beyond our understanding,' said Sherah, as Hatapha, shrugging his shoulders, departed.

'Ah, sister, thou hast that far-away look in thine eyes,' said Ulim.   'Dost thou see beyond what we perceive?'

'I know not.   Some thought rises and yearns within me that I cannot frame, nay, scarce perceive,' replied Sherah; 'but it seems to me that all this—atonement-price, redemption of the first-born—yea, even that intercession and offering of Moses, which was refused as not sufficient—all are meant to convey to us the sense of that great promise of a full price to be paid which Eve dimly understood.'

'Thou ever seest farther than I, sister,' returned Ulim.   'Peace be with thee.'

And Israel dwelt in peace, while the cloud on the mount still remained, though without the former terrific manifestations ; and at last, at the end of the forty days, Moses was seen descending, with the two blocks or tablets of stone in his arms, and with his face bathed in dazzling light, so nearly like the brightness of the sun, that the people fell prostrate, hiding their faces on the ground, or covered them with their burnouses when they tried to look at him.

'He hath borne away somewhat of the Lord's own glory,' said Sherah, veiling her face as she bowed in reverence.

'The glory it is ours to rejoice in,' cried Keren, opening her eyes, which would in spite of herself blink before the sight. And when Moses drew his mantle over his face she still could scarcely see.

'My daughter,' said Sherah, 'such light is not for man to gaze boldly into in this life. Not Moses himself could behold the Lord, and this reflected glory is too much for us weak, blind souls.'

Now that the waiting time was over, Mirglip was urgent for his betrothal to Axa. He had obtained a tent of his own, and a share of his father's kine, goats, and asses was allotted to him; and the parents, therefore, no longer delayed their consent. Dumah and his Keren would share the tents of Sherah, and Mirglip and Axa would be near at hand. The day was fixed when Elishama was to give his blessing solemnly to Axa, and she was to be conducted by her maiden friends to Mirglip's tent. Keren had been blessed and given over to Dumah by her brother, the head of the Izharite clan, and this constituted a valid marriage; but she, too, was to go with Axa to receive the blessing of the head of Mirglip's tribe of Ephraim.

The brides were to be decked in all the splendour that Sherah could muster, most especially that lovely fillet of Asenath, the wife of Joseph, which had been restored to her before the flight. It was to be worn by

Axa over her veil, and no bride was likely to be so well adorned, except by and by when some future daughter of Dumah should grow up to put it on.

While they were still arranging for the brides, Ulim, attended by Adoram, arrived from before the tent of meeting, where the elders had been convened to hear and convey to the people what had been revealed to Moses during the eighty days he had spent on the mysterious summit of the altar mountain.

In the midst of the fiery cloud, entering within the centre, the very Throne of Heaven had been shown to his mortal senses so far as they could receive the idea ; and he was commanded to make what would be a dim shadow, or earthly model, to represent what he had there beheld, to be the symbol of the Lord Jehovah's presence with Israel, and the centre of their worship.

For this, 'for glory and for beauty,' the Israelites were called upon to give their

offerings. The half-shekels offered by the men
were to be used to form the sockets in which
the bars of the tabernacle would be planted to
form the Holy Place, redemption thus becoming the foundation ; and the fabric would be
supported by stakes and boards of shittim
wood or acacia, which abounded around the
camp, and was very enduring.

But much more was required, gold, brass,
precious stones, fine linen, and dainty needle-
work.   Bezaleel, a Levite, and Aholiab, a
Danite, had already been appointed to direct
the work of those who were 'wise hearted'
and had learnt very elaborate and beautiful
arts in Egypt ; and proclamation was made
to the tribes to bring their offerings, and to
undertake handiwork for the service of the
Lord.

Precious stones of the very choicest and
best were wanted for the breastplate of the
High Priest. These were rare among the
Israelites, and Axa looked anxiously at her
mother.   That crown of Asenath !   What

gems it bore in the centre of its lotus flowers!
Ought it not to be offered? Yet might not
Axa wear it once, as a bride only a month
hence? Wear such a crown as no daughter
of Ephraim had ever been seen in? 'Oh,
mother, let me keep it till the wedding!' she
said, 'then the priest shall have it freely.'

'Freely, when thy pride and vanity have
been satisfied! Oh, Axa, thou art a child
still! A month hence and it will be too
late.'

And Axa shed some childish tears ere
she quite made up her mind to surrender the
lovely crown, but by and by the tears were
for her own churlish temper, and she repented
her reluctance as she knelt and laid the golden
wreath before the tent of meeting. Keren,
too, brought her golden ear-rings, and even
Malbeth had a little amulet.

It was a really beautiful sight when woman
after woman deposited her treasures of gold
or of pure white linen, or rich cloths of varied
colours, at the door of the temporary tabernacle

where Moses stood to bless them and the protecting cloud hung above them. Keren was even moved to chant forth a song, in which the other women joined in chorus.

> The daughters of Israel, the wives, and the maidens
> Freely lay their precious things before the Lord,
> Who spoiled their enemies and brought them safe from Egypt.

Sherah was an exquisite embroidress, and to her care were committed the hangings for the sanctuary, stripes of blue, purple (*i.e.* scarlet) and white, to be worked in gold thread with figures of the Cherubim, the fourfold Beings around the Throne, of which dim traditions existed, and two of which were to overshadow the Ark of the Covenant.

Under her, Axa worked obediently and steadily, and so did her cousins in Ulim's tent; but Keren, after she had once puckered the threads up, and been shown that she was spoiling her work, was annoyed. A plain bordering was given her, and then she discovered that it was too hot to sew in the daytime, too dark in the evening, 'and after all, this was so simple that any child could do it!'

'Yes, but for whom is it?' said Axa. 'One stitch for Him is ennobled!'

'And,' added Neria, 'there are directions given out for the neat finish of every border, hems and rings, and taches and all!'

'Doth God take care for them!' exclaimed Keren. 'Is it not only what Moses and Aaron, or maybe Elisheba or Zipporah think well to send forth?'

'Nay,' returned Axa, 'is it not rather thus God would teach us that nought may be heedlessly done which is for His honour, and that even a woman's needle may serve Him in the smallest trifle, so she does it for Him?'

'I can never believe that the great Lord of heaven and earth heeds trifles!' cried Keren.

'And yet He made the beetles,' whispered Axa, looking at a tiny creature, in gemmed armour of green and gold.

Keren surprised them again. There was to be in front of the altar of burnt offering a laver, or brazen vessel in which the priests were to wash before going into the Holy place. Brass was not very frequent among the Israelites, and Miriam had suggested that the women might offer their little hand-mirrors of brightly-polished brass.

Most gave freely, but Keren demurred; she could not do without her mirror. How could she lead the songs of the damsels if her hair were awry, or her veil not straight? It was really not for the honour of worship that she should not appear fit to lead her choir of damsels.

'Would not Dumah's breastplate serve?' asked Axa.

'Dumah's breastplate lengthens one's face and twists the chin and brow. Nay, nay, it is due to all the Ben Beriah that there be one mirror where one can see one's face properly. Moreover, Axa, verily I would yield it up, did I not believe that all this is for the exaltation of the sons of Amram. What have they done to be honoured above all other Kohathites? I speak not of Moses, but Aaron, who led the people in their crime, and his light-minded sons, why should they be honoured above all, and separated from the people, when all are holy ? '

' Nay, child, ask not the *why* of God's own choice,' said Sherah.

Perhaps Sherah was herself surprised, for Korah's family was certainly superior in natural gifts to that of Aaron ; but as she talked it over with Ulim, he observed, ' There is a pride of heart about the sons of Izhar, that would be fed by standing thus forward.'

' A humbled man may serve the Lord more faithfully,' said Sherah.

It was not, however, by Aaron that the brides had to be blessed, but by the head of the tribe, Elishama, who came in state to the tent of Sherah, where Ulim presided over the simple feast. There was very little of cere-mony in the wedding. The bride and bride-

groom stood hand in hand, while the white-
bearded prince pronounced over them the
blessing of faithful marriage, entreating that
they might be like unto Abraham and Sarah,
Isaac and Rebekah, Jacob and Rachel, Joseph
and Asenath, and that they might see their
children's children, and rest in the goodly
land of milk and honey that God reserved
for them.   After this Axa and all the maidens
retired into the women's compartment of the
tent, while the men were waited upon at their
banquet of sheep's flesh, goats' whey, and a
small amount of wine, by the men, and at
midnight the bridegroom, accompanied by
his friends, came for the bride and conducted
her to her new home.

Those two brides and their bridegrooms
were a contrast. Mirglip, calmly and deeply
loving his gentle Axa, with an affection that
had grown up from infancy, and she turning
to him, sweetly, quietly, yet with her whole
nature devoted to him; while Dumah was
a far more eager and vehement lover, proud

of Keren's glorious beauty, and her powers
of song and psalmody, and lavishing every-
thing upon her that heart could devise, and
she accepted, rather than encouraged, his
devotion, with a mind chiefly set on her
beloved brother, his honour and greatness.

CHAPTER XII

A LESSON OF AWE

The Lord breaks out, the unworthy die.
  Lo ! on the cedar floor
The robed and mitred corpses lie ;
  Be silent and adore.
                    KEBLE.

THE months rolled on, and still the camp of
Israel remained in the plain before Mount
Sinai, girdled in by the high mountains
around, which contained many old mines
and smelting furnaces, abandoned by the
Egyptians. There, under the direction of
Bezaleel and Aholiab, the carpenters, gold-
smiths, braziers, spinners, weavers, and
embroiderers were busily employed on the
work of the sanctuary, not a very extensive
edifice in itself, but so exquisitely finished

in every detail as to occupy much time and many hands in the completion.

It was fully six months since the arrival beneath Mount Horeb, when all was finished. The whole had been concealed by the hangings of the outer court, ten feet high, and when at length Moses drew back the curtain from the brazen pillars of the gateway, the spectacle was absolutely dazzling, glittering with bright brass, and further in with gold, and brilliant fresh colours of blue, scarlet, purple, and white, all growing brighter and brighter as the veil of the Holy of Holies was approached, shining with the gold thread worked into it, and with the bright light of the seven lamps of the golden candlestick glancing on it.

Beyond, none could see, but they knew that there was the Ark containing the tables of the Law, overshadowed by the cherubic figures on either side of the mercy-seat, on which rested that intense glory of light above the brightness of the sun, before which even

DISTANT VIEW OF JEBEL-SERBAL, NEAR MOUNT HOREB

Moses could not stand, and which above became the guiding pillar of cloud. They knew that this extreme beauty was the earthly model or miniature of what had been revealed to Moses in Heaven. And before them stood Aaron and his four sons, the anointed priests, the sons in snowy white with coloured sashes or girdles, and caps shaped like the cup of a flower, and Aaron in a beautiful gold-bordered robe of blue, with the breastplate of precious stones, graven with the names of the tribes, and the mitre on his head inscribed with ' Holiness unto the Lord.'

All was intensely beautiful and glorious, yet there was not wanting what was painful in the sacrifices that followed, before the consecration was complete. The blood of bulls and goats must be shed, in token that only through innocent blood could sin be pardoned, and it must be offered by the anointed High Priest standing between the throne and the people.

So Sherah dimly understood, and taught

her daughters and sons during the seven days that completed Aaron's consecration. Axa listened lovingly and receptively, but Keren's heart was burning at having seen *only* Aaron and his sons stand forth. Where were the other Levites? Were Korah and the other Kohathites only to carry the sacred ornaments when they had been taken down and covered up? Why should they be less favoured than those who had not so many personal gifts? Nay, as she could not help believing and murmuring to Axa, these seven days of seclusion, prayer, and sacrifice were like to be an utter weariness to the young men! Why should they be taken when they were not worthy?

'My mother says no one is worthy,' said Axa. 'But these sacrifices are to be instead of our worthiness.'

But Keren was to feel in some degree justified. On the seventh day, fresh sacrifices were offered, burnt offering, sin offering, and peace offering, and with the sacrifice about to be consumed lying on the great brazen altar, Aaron stood forth and solemnly blessed the vast kneeling congregation :

The Lord bless thee and keep thee,
The Lord lift up His face upon thee, and be gracious unto thee,
The Lord lift up His countenance upon thee, and give thee peace.

And as this blessing ended, the glory of the sanctuary shone beyond the veil, and a fire suddenly descended from above and burnt up the offering on the altar!

The people shouted for joy at the acceptance, and fell on their faces.

But Nadab and Abihu, who were perhaps elevated by a hasty draught of wine on their release from the seven days' retirement, had already filled their censers with hot embers of charcoal, and had a certain desire to show off to all the spectators the dignity of their new office. They hurried up to the golden altar of incense in the Holy Place, forgetting or unheeding that the sacred fire alone, which replenished the lamps, was to be used in this immediate service.

One moment, and the fire had leapt forth and, stricken in an instant, they lay dead on the floor of the sanctuary.

In the awe that followed all were speechless. No voice of lamentation was raised, only Moses said, 'This is that which the Lord spake, I will be sanctified in them that come nigh Me, and before all the people I will be glorified.'

Conscious, perhaps, of how little sanctification of spirit and how much irreverence his sons had brought to the outward forms of consecration, Aaron made no reply but knelt as one dumb, while Moses called for two of the Kohathites, and bade them bear the bodies out of the sanctuary as they were, in their white robes, away from the camp, and bury them on the hill-side beyond.

There was to be no mourning by Aaron and his remaining sons, while the holy anointing oil was fresh upon them; but the

whole congregation were to sing dirges
bewailing the sin of their first priests, and
the sudden vengeance that had fallen on
them.

A wild, beautiful chant of mourning echoed
from the rocks around the valley :

> How were the chosen fallen—
> Even with the holy oil on their brow,
> With their white robes all fresh and bright.

So sang the sweet voices, rising up into a
melodious wail, inexpressibly mighty in power,
as it rang out from hill to hill. The Midianites far away looked forth and listened in
wonder at the wailing of the camps of Israel.

Yet Sherah, while mourning for the fall
of the chosen priests, with their consecration
fresh upon them, and feeling it, as did the
brethren forbidden to lament, as a sin on all
the congregation, was grieved to detect in
Keren's lovely voice a note of exultation—
'Aaron's children had been found wanting!'
Others must Moses seek !

CHAPTER XIII

THE MARCH

There rose the choral hymn of praise,
   And trump and timbrel answered keen,
And Israel's daughters poured their lays,
   With priests' and warriors' voice between.

                       SCOTT.

HATAPHA had begun to wonder whether Moses meant to keep Israel on the plain below Mount Sinai for ever, for fresh arrangements and laws continued to be promulgated, many of them on the ceremonial worship, others on the ordinances of the camp, others relating to that promised land, which he said would always be promised, never achieved. Malbeth had given birth to another child, who engrossed her vehement affection so much that little Enhat was left free to paddle about nearly naked in the sand, perfectly happy in the sun. But she shed tears at the thought of her first-born when a second passover was kept, on the anniversary of the first.

It was the prelude to the fresh start of the camp. The princes of each tribe brought their gifts, beginning with six waggons and twelve oxen. These were portioned out among the Levites, to be used in the transport of the tabernacle and its contents. Only the Kohathites received none, as these were to carry the more sacred and precious articles by hand, after the priests had taken them down and prepared them, the Ark itself being carried by the staves fitted to it on the shoulders of four by turns. They had no more close or sacred office, much to the disappointment of Keren, who had fully expected that her brother would have been put in the place of Nadab or Abihu, though Dumah reminded her that there was as much danger as honour in being brought so near. She wondered that the chief of the clan, Elizaphan, did not remonstrate.

She was pleased, however, that when the camp was divided and mapped out, so that each tribe and each section of a tribe knew exactly the position it was to occupy, the Ben Beriah would not be far from the Ben Izhar in the huge parallelogram formed by the camp. For the tribe of Ephraim was at the south-south-west angle of the whole camp, the Kohathites to the south of the Tabernacle.

This sanctuary was the centre of the whole; the four divisions of Levites each had their fixed place around it as guards, and beyond them the other tribes, each with a boundary of its own, and grazing ground for the cattle in the rear.

Each tribe had a banner of its own, the four leading tribes larger and higher than the others. Ephraim had a crimson bullock's head, with golden horns, worked on a purple ground, corresponding to the ligure or jacinth on the high priest's breastplate. It had been

worked by the Ben Beriah with happy songs
on the strength of the bullock.

Judah had a lion on a blood-red ground,
Reuben a man with a water-pitcher on a
lighter red banner, Dan, on the south, an
eagle upon golden yellow; and thus the
four ensigns corresponded to the cherubic
figures.

Ephraim was the leader of the tribes of
Manasseh, Benjamin, and Dan, which formed
the rearguard, and therefore were the last to
move.   The first signal was given by the
rising of the cloud which rested on the Holy
Place.   Then the Levites hastened to take
down and pack the Tabernacle, and the
priests sounded on silver trumpets a summons.
Then, when this eastward division was well
on the way, the cattle collected and driven
on, and the tents raised, another summons
was blown, and the Tabernacle was carried
forward, guarded by Reuben on one side and
Ephraim on the other, Dan going last.   The
Kohathite Levites went after the other

two divisions of their tribe, bearing all that
was most holy shrouded from view.

When the Ark was lifted, Moses gave the
word, and the chant went forth :

Rise up, O Lord, and let Thine enemies be scattered,
And let them that hate Thee flee before Thee.

Keren joyfully took up the song, echoed
from her brothers, and Axa and the other
young matrons and maidens joined in. The
promised land was little more than a week's
journey distant, and Hobab the Midianite
was going on before to point out the best
springs and most suitable camping grounds.

But after the year of rest before Mount
Sinai, the wilderness of Paran seemed very
dreary as the valley of El Tih was entered,
lying between the rocky heights of Edom to
the east and the hills of the Amalekites to
the west. The ground was strewn with
small flints, black and sharp, like bits of
broken glass, the springs were few and far
between, the herbage scanty ; and when little

Enhat strayed into the shade of green retem his mother screamed, for he had nearly been bitten by the venomous horned viper.   It was the noontide halt on the second day's journey.

'Never, never shall we get to the place,' she cried.   'Would that I had stayed behind.'

'Oh no, I would not so,' said Axa, sinking on the mat which Mirglip had spread for her, while he went in search of milk. 'Better to die free than to live a bondswoman!   But die I shall, I must, if this dreadful journey lasts much longer.'

'What say'st thou, my daughter?' said Sherah, coming up. 'Dost thou wax faint and sick-hearted at the very first day of toil and weariness?   Is not the land of milk and honey worth a little hardness and even suffering?'

'Ah, mother! so it may be for those who reach it.'

'And all will reach it who are faithful and

L

patient. Have we not our God for our guide, ever present in yonder cloud? And do we not know Him far better than ever before ? '

'Glory to Him who shone on Mount Sinai!' sang Keren.

And Mirglip here came up with a bowl of goat's milk, which refreshed Axa, so that she cheerfully let him lift her up to her saddle on the ass's back, and, while he walked beside her, she did not think of sighing.

'It is well, she goes on bravely,' said Ulim, coming to the side of Sherah; 'but there may be worse than this to come.'

'These are the first trials that fall on youth,' responded Sherah. 'Well for those who bear them in a good heart, and to whom they are trial enough, as well for those whom they prepare for the heavier proofs that may be in store for them.'

'And seest thou, sister,' said Ulim, 'how for all yesterday's and to-day's tramp over these sharp stones no one is footsore, nor any sandals worn out? It was the same when we journeyed before we came to Sinai —surely a manifest sign of God's hand.'

'Ay,' replied Sherah. 'And after a year's wear our clothes are as fresh as ever. It is as great a marvel as the manna. It is a tender protecting hand that we have over us in yonder cloud.'

'And see, the sun is going down, making purple yonder Amalekite peaks, and the cloud is manifestly resting.'

And therewith the trumpets were sounded, and the chant followed, begun by Moses and taken up by all the Levites—

Return, O Lord, unto the thousands of Israel.

And as the twilight rapidly faded the pillar began to assume a pure and lovely brightness, luminous yet soft—at least in the eyes of Sherah and such as Sherah, who delighted to turn their faces towards it as they said their evening prayer.

But Hatapha and Malbeth looked away

from it.   Malbeth said it was so unnatural
that it terrified her, and Hatapha could not
divest himself of the idea that it was caused
by some magic practices of Moses, who had
learnt so many secrets in his training as an
Egyptian prince.   Some hint of this sort
had made Ulim so angry as to threaten to
take him to Elishama for punishment, and
this silenced him after the first.

Nor were the Ben Beriah much affected
by the disasters which the mixed multitude
brought on themselves by their murmurs.
Hatapha, indeed, let some grumblings escape
him about the fish and the melons of Egypt
and the dulness of this 'light bread,' as the
murmurers called the manna; and when a
second enormous flight of quails descended
upon the camp Malbeth was delighted to
minister to his tastes by cooking for him all
the birds he could possibly eat, and laying
out others, split open, to be dried in the sun
for future consumption.

But even then came the report that those

who had indulged the most in the food, gorged hastily and greedily, were dying of a sudden disease thus caused, and which smote them down in numbers.

Malbeth, in horror, hastened to throw away all she had hoped to preserve ; but every one had tried to dispose of so many that it was almost impossible to escape from reminders of them.   Hatapha, and even little Enhat, were both ill, though both recovered as soon as the camp moved away from this melancholy spot, which is still marked in the wilderness as the 'Graves of them that lusted.'

The 'light bread' was physically the most wholesome food in the heated atmosphere; and, though all did not feel, like Ulim, Sherah, and their children, that it was to be eaten in reverence as heavenly meat, it was certain that those who lived on it obediently throve upon it.   Yet the quails were not in themselves poisonous, as poor Malbeth fancied, for the young men and women had eaten of them, but in moderation, and had been unhurt.

'To enjoy the gift of God is one thing,' said Sherah, 'to lust and be discontented is another.'

CHAPTER XIV

THE GOODLY LAND

Now (Israel) hold your own, the land before you
Is open. Win your way, and take your rest.
So sounds our war note.
                    KEBLE.

THE steep uphill struggle ended in a rest at
Ain Kadesh (the well of Kadesh), on an
upland plain, thickly interspersed with retem
or white broom, full of good pasture. The
well or spring from which it was named
came gushing out of a cliff frowning above
the plain. A ridge of mountains lay to the
east, and it was known that to the west the
host of Amorites were awaiting the Israelites.
The Negeb, or south country, was within a
couple of days' journey. They were at the
very gates of the glorious land of promise.

'So near!' cried Keren. 'Methinks I can smell the balmy gales, as the soft wind wafts them to us!'

'One brave effort,' added Dumah. 'The Amorites are broken like the Amalekites, and we are in the land of our fathers, our labours over!'

'Only to be brave in the strength of the Lord!' said Mirglip, who was polishing his breastplate.

'Yea, my son, I would that we were thus to go forward with a good heart,' said Ulim, who had just come in from Moses' tent; 'but the elders speak the voice of the tribes when they demand that spies should be sent first to explore the country.'

'Explore!' cried Keren; 'cannot they trust the Lord to give us what is good?'

'The men who were once taken on the campaign of Pharaoh tell stories of dangerous passes and cities fenced up to Heaven,' said Ulim, 'and the hearts of some of the people are daunted so that they require of

Moses to send scouts before them to discover how it is with the land.'

'Better to go straight on in the might of the Lord,' said Sherah. 'If He be for us, who can be against us?'

'Even so, sister; but unless we have trust in Him He will not be on our side. And alas! there are many whose spirit is so bowed down by their past bondage that they would fear and fly instead of standing up steadfast in His might.'

'And who are to go?' asked Sherah anxiously.

'I hope I may,' said Mirglip. 'I long to see Hebron and the cave of Machpelah and Shechem, where our father Joseph is to lie.'

'There will be only one man of each tribe,' said his father. 'So will they better be able to avoid observation.'

Mirglip and Dumah were disappointed; so was Keren; but Axa breathed more freely, however, when Joshua was selected as the representative of Ephraim. He found

that each chief spy might take with him a
few light-footed young men, and his choice
fell on the two cousins, Adoram and Dumah.
They departed toward the southward so as
to avoid the mountain in front, where the
Amorites were on the watch for them, meaning to make a detour, and enter where they
would be only viewed as ordinary desert
wanderers, such as continually prowled among
the numerous detached nations of Palestine.

All the time of their absence the pillar of
cloud remained stationary, and the camp
rested at Kadesh-Barnea, and there it was
that their first-born son was born to Mirglip
and Axa.   They did not circumcise him;
that ceremony was put off until the entrance
into the Holy Land.   The proud young
father, Mirglip, called him Zuriel, meaning
' My rock is God.'

In due time the spies were hailed as returning, travel-worn and dusty, but bearing
in their hands beautiful bunches of heavily-
eared corn, and on the shoulders of their

attendants poles with enormous bunches of grapes.

' The firstfruits of the land,'

sang Keren, as she danced out to meet her husband who turned his steps to the tents of his family, while Joshua and the other chiefs went to make their report to Moses.

Korah came in to hear the report of the two young men, for Levi being now separate had not sent out a delegate, Manasseh being taken in their stead. Like true Eastern story-tellers, Adoram and Dumah sat in the midst. All the family sat round upon the ground listening—Sherah, Zillah, and the other women waiting on them as they partook of the kid of welcome, only Axa remaining within hearing behind the curtain of the tent, as the days of her seclusion were not accomplished.

It was a tale to be listened to with enthralling eagerness, as Dumah told how, turning to the south, they had climbed into the long, gradually-rising defile belonging to the children of Edom. 'They dwell all along those hills in dens and caves of the rock, carved on the face, and hollowed into dwellings within.'

'Were they at peace with you?'

'Yes, they treated us well. They owned us for brethren, and I think they hate the Amorites as much as we do. They sold us bread and wine, and let us drink of their wells, and thus ascending, by and by we looked down as into a pit, where lay the bluest of all blue seas.'

'What!' exclaimed Sherah; 'is it that Sea of Salt where lie the wicked cities that were overwhelmed with fire and brimstone?'

'Even so, mother. So Joshua told us.'

'And can that be blue?'

'So it was, bluer even than the Great Sea we have sometimes seen in Egypt; but when we descended by a mountain path and would have bathed in it, the water was so thick and heavy that we could not sink. Nor was

there a fish to be seen within them, nor
a bird above them, and dead trunks and
branches of trees lay about the banks among
lumps of salt and pitch (bitumen).

'We shall ever be kept in mind of God's
judgment,' said Sherah.

'True,' said Dumah; 'for when I gathered
a fair round fruit, growing like an apple, and
would have eaten it, it crushed into ashes
which filled my mouth.'[1]

'Is that the land filled with milk and
honey?' said Hatapha.

'Nay, listen, Hatapha. We went up
again, the salt of that sea making us ready to
die with thirst all the way, through the low
hills of Moab. When we halted at a
spring and for pity's sake asked for a
drink, the shepherds laughed us to scorn as
strangers who had had the folly to taste of
the bitter waters.'

'Did they let you quench your thirst?'

'Ay, for our sheikhs paid them for the

[1] Probably the 'apple of Sodom' is an oak gall.

draught, and we were too many and too well armed for them to attack, but we made the best of our way onwards lest they should summon their king and his warriors, and pretend that we had been stealing their flocks of well-fed sheep which graze all over the pasture lands.   So we forded the brook Jabbok, which may be a torrent in the winter but is a mere chain of pools in the summer, and came down to the valley of the Jordan. The river rushes along between banks covered thick with trees and bushes.   Joshua and Caleb of Judah said they would not wish for a better defence to guard our land.'

'Yes, when we are in it!' said Hatapha; 'and pray how did you get over this flood?'

'We traced it towards the source, cutting down the thorns and tangles as we went, and ever and anon killing a roebuck for our meat, or some of the ducks that haunted the rushes.   We had to be on our guard, for in the holes of the cliffs there were dens of lions and leopards.   Caleb had a sharp battle

with a young lion, ere he could kill it with
his axe.   He wears the skin, and we tell him
it is in honour of the Lion of Judah.   Thus
we came to Bethbarah, the House of Passage,
where there is a ford, but there is a fenced
city of the Amorites, and we thought it
wiser to go farther north.   Before us we
saw two great white peaks rising up into the
sky, that we thought at first were clouds.'

'White!'

'Ay, some said it was snow, which
we could hardly believe.   And by and by,
beneath us lay, as we went through the oak
woods, another fair lake, blue and beauteous,
with a white fringe around it.   We doubted
of drinking lest it should be salt, but it was
fair, pure, and delicious to the taste, and
the people who lived about it said that it
abounded in fish.'

'Fish!' sighed Hatapha; 'I have not
seen fresh-water fish since I left Egypt.'

'Well, they seemed to be plentiful there,
and the people were Canaanites, quiet folk

who dwelt in farms and gardens, and were subject to the great city of Zidon on the seashore.'

'Whence come ships to Eygpt from time to time,' said Ulim.

'Ay, so it was; and save that once we saw a horrid valley, with a furnace in the midst, where they make their children pass through the fire to a frightful god whom they call Moloch, these country folk were simple and peaceable. They took us for wild children of the East, and set all we needed before us, being only amazed that we paid for what we had. Thus did we cross the river, beyond the lake where it becomes shallow and beset with such papyrus reeds as we knew in Egypt. Above us was that snowy height, and on the hills that rose around, such trees as never were seen in Egypt. Cedars of Lebanon they were called, and we were told that we only saw the utmost part of them, and could not guess at their size and beauty. Trees that never lose their leaves and have fragrant wood that brooks no worm nor decay.'

'Cedar - wood, ay, the Zidonian merchants tow beams and rafts thereof to Egypt,' said Ulim.

'And all this to be ours!' said Mirglip.

'Nay, there is better still. We went on, turning southwards, through hills less high sloping down to the lake, woodland and pasture ground, delightsome to those who shall dwell there. And to the westward, on our right hand, whenever the hills or the woods opened enough, we could see glimpses of the great wide sea. So we went on day after day, till, shut in by the ridges of hills, we beheld a rich cornfield, waving for the harvest, spreading out wide and rich, the surface only broken by some lesser hills, or by the walls of a city. There was one city close to two steep hills, one a cliff, the other a fair smiling slope into the valley rich with fruit-trees, vineyards, and waving corn ; and Joshua bade us Ephraimites look at it well,

M

for this was Shechem which our father Jacob
bequeathed to ourselves.'

'And where Joseph's bones are to rest,'
said Ulim.

'It is indeed a goodly heritage,' added
Adoram; 'greener and richer than Egypt,
not trusting to the overflow of the river and
the labour of men to guide the channels, but
to the rain from heaven coming down in
streams from the mountain-side.'

'Our home!' said Sherah; 'soon to be
our rest! One or two labours more!'

'And we shall be sitting under our vine
and fig-tree,' cried Keren joyfully.

'How was it with the people of the place?'
demanded Ulim.

'They are Hivites and Hittites, split up
into many little kingdoms,' returned Adoram;
'but as far as we could understand, they are
all united at the camp of the Amorites to
withstand our passage. One sharp fight and
then all is ours!'

'God befriending us,' said his father.

'And that will be our home!' said Mirglip.   'Hearest thou, Axa?'

'Our home and thine, my little Zuriel!'
responded Axa from within.

'Tell on,' entreated Keren.   'Dumah, my
husband, hast thou chosen thine house?'

'I saw a house with a vine o'ershadowing
the porch that made me think of thee,' replied
Dumah.   'More than once did I hope to
choose our dwelling-place, as we went on
for three days' journey, past the very spot
where our forefather Joseph was seized by
his brethren and thrown into the pit.'

'The pit was there—a cistern, no doubt
sometimes dry, but we drank from it,' added
Adoram, 'and thought of the weary journey
of our father into Egypt.'

'Then the ground rose again, higher,
steeper still,' continued Dumah, 'and each
hill was crowned with a watch-tower or a
city, with a king of its own.   God must have
helped us, or we could never have got
through so many enemies.'

'Yea, we ever found either cottages left empty, or else friendly fellaheen, who told us our way. It was from them that we knew that the high hill that rose above a circle of lesser ones was Mount Moriah, whither Abraham led his son for sacrifice, but it is now held by the Jebusites and Adonizedek, their fierce king, and they call it Jebus.

'It was the dwelling of Melchizedek, to whom Abraham gave the tithe of the spoil,' observed Ulim, who was well taught in the records and traditions of his forefathers.'

'So said Joshua, and then Caleb looked up to the point as it lifted its head and hoped that there would dwell his people. He thought of it all along the slopes, down from the hill country, all covered with vineyards, and whenever we passed a specially fine one, in his gruff warrior's voice he would sing the song of Jacob's death-bed :

'Binding his foal unto the vine
And his ass's colt unto the choice vine,
He washed his garments in wine,
And his clothes in the blood of grapes.'

'Was it from thence that ye brought the cluster of enormous grapes?' asked Ulim.

'That was from Eshcol, nigh unto Hebron.'

'Hebron! the special resting-place of our fathers in life or death!' said Sherah.

'Yea, mother. There we saw the oak of Mamre still growing and green, and the field of Machpelah, with the cave where, far within the inner recess, lie the tombs of Abraham and Sarah, of Isaac and Rebekah, of Jacob and Leah, far away from the ridge hill of Ephrath, where lies Rachel our mother. But, while we were praying around the cave, Gaddi of Manasseh and Shammua of Reuben had such a fright that I know not if they will ever recover it, for upon them, out of Hebron, there came a party of sons of Anak, as much bigger than we as a crocodile of the Nile is than one of these little lizards of the desert. In their terror they cried out aloud, and ran up to hide themselves in our midst. But they were friendly giants, who laughed at their fears, and when they knew that we were sons of Abraham, they owned our claim to the field, and left us un-molested. Their two sheikhs, the biggest of them all, were called Sheshai and Talmai. They sat down with us and told us that there was an old prophecy that the children of Abraham, the Friend, should possess the land, but they did not seem in the least afraid of such little beings as we must have seemed to them. Indeed, the great sheikhs wanted to buy the Egyptian girdle that Ammiel brought from the Red Sea shore, so it was given, and a few other matters, and in return they sent us a fat sheep, and let us cut down the grapes. Caleb was quite friendly with them, and said, when they were gone, that they would be goodly foes to fight with.'

'Joy! joy!' sang Keren. 'The gates of our land are open to us! The Lord our God will bring us in, as He sware unto our fathers! Joy! joy!'

'Joy! joy!' echoed her brother; 'our sword shall win our home. To the battle and the victory. Bring forth your cymbals. We will make this our war song to-morrow!'

CHAPTER XV

Because we would not onward press
When close to Zion's hill.
KEBLE.

KORAH and Keren were still chanting their
song, with bright eyes lighted up with hope,
when a tremendous shouting and yelling was
heard, mixed with sounds of execration.
Rushing out, they found the whole camp in a
dire state of confusion, anger, and lamentation.
The Levite guard was striving to keep back
the men, who seemed perfectly maddened as
they rushed with terrific howls and cries of
despair upon the enclosure round the Tabernacle. In front of it stood Caleb, and with
him Joshua, whose aged grandfather, Elishama, stood near, brave but grieved, and

holding out a hand to his kinsman, Ulim, sighed to him, 'Alas! alas! these faint-hearted spies! They have infected the whole of this faithless, foolish people!'

Caleb, standing on a stone, a tall, vigorous, upright figure, was trying to make himself heard. 'Ye foolish sheep—worse than your own sheep! No wolf is nigh. There lies the land! We have but to go in. We are well able to overcome those men! The Lord is among us! Who need be afraid? Cowards that ye are!'

Caleb's voice, though a strong one, and animated by hot indignation, was unheard or disregarded amid the yells that rang out: 'Down with him! Down with him! 'Tis a plot to get us all killed in the wilderness! Traitor!'

Joshua, stretching out his spear, tried to speak, but his voice too was drowned amid the execrations and lamentations of the people, and it was all the Levite guard could do to keep the throngs from bursting in on the space around the Tabernacle, in front of which Moses and Aaron stood waving them back with menacing gestures, which seemed only to increase their rage.

The deep darkness of night, however, fell on them, and dispersed them. The sanctuary light was now a red and angry spark, which afforded no illumination, and the people retired as best they could to their tents ; but all through that night the air resounded with the clamorous bewailings of the East, mourning for themselves and their children, dragged forth to be the prey of their cruel enemies. Ulim and his sons with Joshua went about to try to silence this recreant spirit, but they found that though their own tribe of Ephraim was fairly staunch, yet Gaddi, Ammiel, and the rest had infected the multitude with their own cowardice. The giants had in their imagination grown to five times their height, and were waiting on their crags to devour the little children, whose mothers were wailing over them as certain victims. They were crying out to be led back to Egypt, and among the men there were angry whispers and mutterings as if they were planning to rise against Moses and force a return to Egypt. Daggers were drawn against those who withstood them, and save for the darkness, Ulim could hardly have escaped from an angry blow aimed at him by a Benjamite with whom he was arguing.

He came back melancholy and dispirited at this faithless requital of God's favours, the effect of those years of slavery which had so dejected the spirit of the Israelites that they could not be nerved to an exertion of courage. It was with them as it has often been with enslaved nations, they were altogether demoralised ; and after all the wonders that had been worked for them, and in which they were living, they could not take heart to confront the natives of the land, nor be-lieve any assurance of protection. The men left the women and children to gather the

daily allowance of manna, and spear in hand
rallied in front of their tents, some of the
sheikhs coming forward in consultation, and
proposing to make Shammua, the Reubenite,
captain of the host by right of birth, and to
turn back to Egypt.

Ephraim's tents were on a little rising
ground, and thence the women could plainly
see the tumultuous party gathered round, and
the ensign of Reuben, the red banner with
the water-bearer, borne to the midst.

'Unstable as water, thou shalt not excel,'
repeated Sherah.   'Reuben, thou hast never
been worthy to be the first-born.'

'Look,' cried Keren, 'there are Caleb and
Joshua with rent garments rushing among
them.   See their hands waving, their angry
gestures.   Strike the cowardly recreants
down, brave Caleb.   Ah! they are seizing
them, dragging them out.   Where are Korah
and the Levite guard?'

'I see, father,' exclaimed Neria, 'he is
trying to reason with them,' she added as

Eastern gesticulation was thoroughly apparent. ‘He is throwing himself between——’

‘Ah! ah!’ screamed Keren, ‘they are seizing him too! Where are the Levite guard? Where is that laggard Aaron?’

‘The Reubenites are crowding up! Oh! what a yell!’

‘They are breaking through the Levites.’ Sherah stood with clasped hands looking upward, not gazing at her son and brother in their imminent danger, while the young wives and maidens shrieked around her.

‘There's a wretch heaving a stone! Oh! Alas! alas! He is aiming it at Caleb. Ah!’

At that moment the cloud upon the Tabernacle became one sheet of awful lightning, darting to and fro—indescribably terrible. Every one in the congregation, victims and their enemies alike, fell down on their faces, unable to bear the insufferable wrathful glare of light.

An awful stillness succeeded. Only Sherah, venturing to lift up her eyes, saw that Moses was kneeling before the door of the Holy Place, one figure enveloped in the strange brightness around.

Later, it was known how urgently he pleaded, in anguish of heart, as it was set before him that the whole perverse faithless people should be consumed on the spot, and himself left alone, to become the father of a new race in whom the promise should be fulfilled. Was it a temptation, or rather was it to be the means of his again being the mediator and intercessor for his people, so rebellious yet so beloved, when he pleaded that it was not for the honour of God Himself, after bringing them thus far, to let them perish in the wilderness; pleading, too, God's own proclamation of His mercy in the wondrous manifestation at Sinai ?

Pardon was won for the nation, but not exemption from chastisement, and betokening this, lightnings flashed out from that terrific glory, and, with unerring aim, fell upon each of the ten faithless spies who had spread the evil report, and then inflamed the cowardly violence of the mob. Shammua, Palti, Gaddi, Ammiel, and the rest, all lay dead by a sudden stroke or flame, blackened corpses—Shammua grasping the banner of Reuben, Palti and Gaddi holding the stones they had been about to aim at Caleb and Joshua, who stood upright and safe, though greatly awe-struck. Ulim with the others of the seventy elders repaired to the Tabernacle, there to hear the will of the Lord, as revealed to Moses, and then to be made known each to his own section of the tribe.

He came back to the tents of the Ben Beriah weeping as he went and with bowed head. All gathered round to hear, in how different a mood from the exultation of the evening before! As usual, Keren was the first to spring forth and ask if they were pardoned, and might go on, now that those evil men had fallen. Surely he was not mourning for them, any more than for Nadab and Abihu.

'Nay, child, I mourn for all, for the sin of all this perverse congregation. It was not only the spies who erred, but the whole mass of the people, all Israel who, after all the marvels that He hath done, refuse to trust Him, or to go forward when He goes before them. Therefore hear His decree that He hath spoken to Moses. None of us that were men when we came out of Egypt, none over twenty years of age, save Joshua and Caleb alone, shall go into the land of Canaan. Silence, Hatapha! Peace, Adoram! Keren, my daughter, wail not aloud. I know not if this touches our women. Nor is there to be a sudden destruction, but the land we would not strive for, we are not to enter. We are to turn back into the wilderness of Zin and tarry there forty years, one year for each day of spying the land, till one by one all the elders have died, and the young, the little ones, shall have grown up in a braver, freer temper to possess the land of promise.'

'Thou, thou, father,' exclaimed Mirglip;

'thou, who taught us to look for the land and feel it our own, surely thou wilt be excepted!'

His daughters and wife hung round him weeping bitterly, and their sobs and tears were echoed by the dwellers in the tents around.

'Nay, children,' said Ulim, 'weep for the sin of Israel, but weep not for me. I am content to live as my forefathers, Abraham, Isaac, and Israel have lived before me, in tents, looking onward to the promise to their children.'

'Yea,' added Sherah, 'you, my sons and daughters, and little Zuriel, yours will be the inheritance.'

'Assuredly,' said Ulim, 'to them is the promise. Nor was aught said of women, sister, and thou, Keren. It was on the men of twenty years old who were numbered that the doom fell.'

'And Levi was not numbered,' eagerly exclaimed Keren. 'So my brothers are safe, as well they merit.'

N

'And who should lead the way into the land save Moses and Aaron!' exclaimed Zillah. 'But thou, my lord and husband, thou art blameless in all this! Will not the Lord hear our prayer for thee?'

'Thou forgettest, my good Zillah, there is work for me to do for the Lord, in striving to train the young ones to be fit to conquer the land. That is enough for me in this world. Canaan is not the only rest.'

'No,' said Sherah, 'there is a rest beyond.'

CHAPTER XVI

SELF-WILL

Lest . . . .
War terrify them, inexpert, and fear
Return them back to Egypt, choosing rather
Inglorious life with servitude, for life
So noble and ignoble, is more sweet
Untrained in arms, where rashness leads not on.

MILTON.

SUCH submission as that of Ulim was not universal. There was a gathering of the more warlike in the evening. Both Hatapha and Adoram were there, and came back resolved to insist upon being led against the enemy according to the original plan. Ulim was absent and they spoke out freely.

'Why should we attend to the outcry of those miserable cowards?' declared Adoram, 'we who have seen that beauteous land of hill and valley.   Joshua and Caleb are right. One effort, and it is done.'

'One effort, but with the Lord,' said his brother.

'The Lord will be with us if we go on valiantly,' said Dumah.

'Not without Him.   Not contrary to His word,' hesitated Mirglip.

'His word!' said Hatapha.   'Say rather that Aaron is flinching at the last and carrying Moses along with him.'

'As I knew he would,' exclaimed Keren, who had much freedom of speech for one so young, in right of her Kohathite birth and gift of poetry (or prophecy).

'Sister, sister, it was the Lord who manifested himself,' said Neria.

'We none of us know Moses' power over appearances,' said Hatapha, 'nor his plausibility in explaining them.   Remember, he was bred among Egyptian priests and magicians.'

Ulim would have silenced these evil

suggestions instantly, but the younger people listened, and not without effect, and Hatapha went on to dwell on the unreasonableness of leading the multitude back into the desert. It was plain, he declared, that whatever the two brothers had hoped or intended on leaving Egypt, the report of the spies had daunted their courage and they were delaying, under pretext of divine commands, to make the decisive attack. Unless the braver warriors nerved themselves to begin the war of invasion and conquest, they would all be taken back into the wilderness and become a mere wandering tribe, like the sands of the desert, forgetting all the arts of life that they had brought from Egypt, and with Moses, or his son Gershom, as sheikh over them, and Aaron and his sons as their priestly caste. Now was the time for action! And at that moment there was a trumpet-call. Not the blast on the silver trumpet that called the tribes to prepare for movement, but sharper and more peremptory,

and the wolf ensign of Benjamin was seen
moving towards the camp of Ephraim.
Two warriors, with brazen helmets and
shields, rushed forward crying, 'Up, men
of Ephraim! Yours was the brave report!
We will not bear with being driven back
like silly sheep! Abidan is our leader.
We will fall upon the Amorites and smite
them as we smote the Amalekites.'

Nothing more was wanting. Hatapha,
Adoram, Mirglip, and Dumah each hurried
into his tent to don helmet and breastplate,
and take up his shield and spear. Keren
was ready to arm Dumah, glad that his
mother was absent, for round Adoram were
clinging Zillah and her daughters, entreating
him to wait till his father returned, and
Mirglip found his wife, Axa, being arrayed
by her mother Sherah to go up to the
Tabernacle for her purification on the fortieth
day, the lamb tied to the tent pole, and the
infant Zuriel lying in the arms of his smiling mother the silver half-shekel for his

redemption lying ready for Mirglip to present.

'It must be done without me,' cried the youth. 'There is a call to arms!'

'A call to arms!' said Sherah, moving to the door of her tent. 'I heard no alarm on the silver trumpets! The cloudy pillar moves not.'

'Nay, but our people have determined to show that we are not so faint of spirit as those miserable spies pretended. We are going to rush forth and prove ourselves worthy.'

'Worthy of what?' demanded Sherah. 'Of the punishment of God?'

'Of His help and blessing,' muttered Mirglip less confidently.

'Oh no, no, Mirglip, my beloved husband,' cried Axa. 'Go not forth. No victory can attend those who have no blessing. Thou wilt be lost to this babe, thy first-born, and to me. Stay, oh stay, till we learn the will of God.'

'Adoram is arming, and Dumah, and Hatapha, and all the rest ; I cannot be kept back from a brave effort. We never believed that evil report. We never feared the giants. Why should not our valour bring a recall of the sentence ? ' said Mirglip, trying to shake off his weeping wife, who was striving to take away his spear, and put the child in his arms instead.

'Because,' said Sherah, 'when God has spoken of a chastisement it is our duty to submit.'

And as she saw her own son, Dumah, at the door of her adjacent tent, with a shining spear in his hand and his bow behind him, she stepped forward and said, 'Lay down those arms, my son. Thou wilt but wail with shame and disgrace if thou goest in defiance of our Lord God.'

'Nay,' cried Keren, running forth. 'He never was a coward. We never hung back. Why listen to the weak alarms of Aaron and turn back when all is before us ? '

'Peace and silence, daughter. Dumah, I command thee.'

'Mother, I cannot be branded as a recreant coward,' said Dumah. 'Women's entreaties,' and he looked scornfully at his sister hanging on Mirglip, 'should not hold a warrior back! Keren knows better and sends me forth in my might.'

'But not in the might of the Lord,' said Sherah. 'Is it so long since thou hast heard in His own voice, " Honour thy father and thy mother?"'

'And oh, Mirglip,' was Axa entreating, 'think how thou wouldst feel if this little one, because he would not submit to thy chastisement, did the very thing thou hadst forbidden.'

'Are ye coming, brothers?' exclaimed Adoram coming out fully armed and joining Hatapha, who was splendid in Egyptian armour. Zillah, her daughters, and Malbeth, were all in a passion of weeping, calling on them to come back and save their lives, in

pity to their children, and appealing to Sherah
to forbid them.   Indeed, Zillah had de-
spatched little Zemira in search of his father,
and in good time.   Ulim, in his flowing
robes, staff in hand, was coming towards
them, over the space in front of the tents.

'What is this, children?' said his powerful voice.   'What tumult is this?   Would
you bring on yourselves the wrath of God?'

'Father, they are gone!' cried Mirglip.
'Let us go.   We never feared!   We shall
bring back the favour of God, destroy
the Amalekites—win the land by our sword
and spear.'

'Not by perverse disobedience,' said
Ulim.   'Elishama forbids in the name of
Moses.   Lay down your weapons, faithful
Ben Beriah.   Give up your spears, my
sons.'

Mirglip and Dumah obeyed, but Keren
wept bitterly over the command, and both
Hatapha and Adoram, as soon as they
discerned Ulim's figure approaching, had

hastened onwards to join Abidan and the Wolf of Benjamin, together with a confused number of Ephraimites as well as of other tribes, whom their chieftains had, some permitted to go, some endeavoured to keep back, according to their spirit of faith and submission, or of perverse daring. They were in fact all the most lawless and adventurous spirits of the camp, half Bedouin in their habits and dispositions, who did not fully believe in the inspiration of Moses, or on whose light minds warnings made slight impression.

Ulim would not let his remaining sons or followers run to call them back lest they too should be swept away by the disorderly multitude, whose shrill blasts upon the horns of rams and kine, and wild war-songs, came back to them on the breeze.

Ulim turned to Mirglip and Axa, and said, endeavouring to be cheerful, while Mirglip leant on his spear, sobbing without restraint, 'Come, mine obedient son. The blessing of God is on thy submission. Thou shalt see the goodly land, thou and this little one, on whom rests the blessing of God won by a dutiful father.   Cheer you, my sons, ye will have plenty of occasion for courage in the cause of the Lord.'

Mirglip, who was still a mere boy, though already a father, cheered up as best he might under the commendation, though much disappointed, and the little procession set forth, Dumah and Keren turning aside by the wish of the latter to hear what her brother Korah thought.   The camps seemed silent and empty as they went along, and Korah, who stood near his tent polishing a breastplate, greeted them by saying, 'That is well, Dumah, thou art not gone forth with that foolish people.'

'Thinkest thou them foolish?' exclaimed Keren.   'Only old Ulim's command and Sherah's withheld my lord Dumah.'

'It was well done,' returned Korah. 'As I have been telling Dathan and Abiram, this is no time for an attack on the banded nations in yonder mountain, by our tumultuary people. They need time for hands and hearts to be trained for war.'

'But thou art sharpening thy weapons!'

'Yea; it may be that all our valour may be needed, all our most fierce spirits being gone, in case their flight bring down an attack of the foe upon the camp. Then, Dumah, thou wouldst have fighting enough to prove thee. Phinehas has been with us to bid us look to our arms. Oh yes, Moses is a prudent leader, whether his inspiration be from man or from the sanctuary.'

CHAPTER XVII

THE ROUT AT HORMAH

Nor yet their fathers' footsteps trace,
A froward and disloyal race,
    A race infirm of heart :
Of soul to God untrue, they turned,
Even Ephraim, when the battle burned,
    Though armed with bow and dart.
           OXFORD PSALTER.

THE purifying, with the offering of the lamb, was over, and likewise the presentation of the first-born son, redeeming him by the half-shekel, and the young mother, fair, modest, and lovely, knelt on under her veil, to receive the blessing of Aaron, while her mother, gifted with a far-seeing, yearning spirit, gazed on, as though she saw beyond the gold-worked curtain of the Holy Place to one perfect and sufficient atonement-

price of which the half-shekel was but the
type.

Mirglip stood waiting, obeying his father,
but not wholly consoled for the loss of the
enterprise he longed after, when the young
priest Phinehas laid a hand on his arm.
'Where are thy brothers?' he said.

'Adoram is gone forth with the host,' said
Mirglip wistfully; 'I remain by my father's
command.'

'That is well,' replied Phinehas. 'Fetch
thy weapons, Mirglip. If these stiff-necked
fellows provoke the Amalekites, we must
show a bold front, and be ready to hinder
them from attacking the camp.'

'It is well,' responded Ulim, as the glad
light flashed into his son's dark eye; 'Joshua
is already gone to collect such valiant men as
have remained within the camp in obedience
to the voice of the Lord, and to post watch-
men and guards.'

The Amorites and Amalekites were
posted on a hill only twenty miles distant,

around a watch-tower and city called at that
time Zephath; and though hitherto they
had been withheld, no doubt by divine
Providence, from attacking the Israelite
camp, it was in the natural order of things
that a disorderly assault on them would
bring them down in pursuit; and though the
protection of God over His people was
certain, yet none could tell that it might
only be vouchsafed as the result of hard
fighting of their own accompanied by
disasters that might carry out part of the
doom pronounced in the sentence, denuded
too as the camp was of the most recklessly
brave and warlike, who had fought in the
Egyptian wars.

Thus the elder men gravely, and the
younger ones cheerfully, prepared for defence, at least all those who justified the
decision that they were unfit to be conducted
against the inhabitants of Palestine, for they
either were indifferent to the summons of
Joshua, Caleb, and Phinehas, or they de-

clared that it would be useless to defend themselves, and began to strike their tents and prepare for flight.

The north-eastern tribes, Judah and Dan, were the nearest to the enemy, and it was the Danites, always an adventurous tribe with many strong men in it, who had poured forth in large numbers, together with the Reubenites and Benjamites from the south. Judah, however, was in force under the Lion, and Caleb was in command here with the waggons drawn up so as to form a sort of barricade. Joshua was commanding the entire muster, and watching over the sentries whom he had posted on all sides, and sent to direct the bringing in of the cattle which were grazing in the rear of every tribe, while Phinehas marshalled the Levite guard of the Tabernacle.

Ulim, a stout and resolute man, found his thousand of the tribe of Ephraim fairly responsive to the call, though too many had gone, like Adoram and Hatapha. Elishama

called them over, name by name, and one
out of three was missing at his summons;
but as Ephraim and Gad formed the rearguard, and an attack was not to be expected
there, Elishama permitted the men of the
Ben Beriah to go forward and reinforce
Caleb in the front.

Even as they went, Mirglip, who was
keen of eye, could point out in the clear
transparent atmosphere, on the steep hill
that rose from the ravine between them and
Zephath tower, the dark masses of Israelites,
struggling upwards, but all in scattered
irregular form, not in the close array on
which Joshua would have insisted.

The noonday sun began to flash on their
spear-points, but it flashed on something
more sinister on the heights above them, on
other spears and breastplates, and therewith
on a close, heavy, darting kind of cloud.
'Arrows!' said Caleb; 'oh, my brethren!' as
it descended on them.

For some minutes nothing could be seen,

but then it was plain there was a general
mêlée, the enemy probably hurling themselves down on the too-confident assailants.
The fight lasted for some time before the
whole mountain-side was like an ant-hill,
alive with rushing forms, utterly confused,
and small as insects at such a distance, but
alas! there could be no doubt as to who
were the defeated.

The mountain-side was still covered with
figures, probably of the slain and the
plunderers, when fugitives began to come
panting up the near side of the ravine,
pursued by parties of long-haired, long-
speared enemies. Each unhappy runaway
seemed to have a swarm of wild horsemen
following him, with streaming hair and
burnouse, chasing them 'as bees do,' as
Moses long after described the sight. Caleb
called out the stoutest of his men beyond
the barricade, there to stand firm, shoot at
the pursuers with their bows, or throw their
long darts and thus save the fugitives, never

breaking their ranks, and turn back the pursuit. Some were saved in this manner, for the little Arab horses, though swift and sure-footed, were blown with the ascent of the steep side of the ravine, and the hail of missiles disconcerted their riders, so that safety was won by such as could reach the top of the steep rocky side, unless the pursuers were especially well mounted.

Mirglip suddenly saw Adoram, bleeding, but still struggling forward. He had surmounted the bank of the ravine, but two horsemen and three runners were close on him, armed, happily, only with swords or daggers, having exhausted their missiles. Mirglip, calling out in despair to Caleb, 'My brother, my brother! I must defend him,' launched his javelin, striking one rider in the neck, and then darting forward; but the slight, lithe lad would have been instantly struck down among the four remaining enemies, had not Caleb rushed forward to his rescue with Dumah at the same moment.

An arrow from Ulim laid low the foremost of the running men just as he had his hand on Adoram's shoulder, one swing of Caleb's heavy club overthrew the other horseman, and the struggle with the two remaining Amalekites was brief. Adoram, exhausted and bleeding, was supported by the two youths back to the lines, where his father received him, and Caleb, shaking his head at Mirglip, with a sort of grim good-humour, said, 'Boy, boy, thou madest me break my line! How shall we punish thee, or how shall we meet Joshua? Thy father better understood war!'

Ulim and Dumah were kneeling on the ground attending to Adoram. A dart had torn his side, and an arrow had pierced his arm, but neither seemed to be a fatal wound, and when some water had been given him and he could speak, he told them that Hatapha had been cut down by his side, and that none of the Israelites had been able to stand for a moment against the Amorites and Amalekites.

'I have sinned against the Lord, and against thee, O my father!' he sighed. 'Carry me to my mother,' he added faintly.

As Ulim gave the kiss of peace in assurance of pardon, Joshua, a grand and noble figure in his bright helmet and cuirass, approached. The pursuit seemed to be at an end. Though still worn out, sometimes wounded survivors crept in, especially after dark, such as had fallen by the way and been left for dead, or who had hidden themselves behind rocks or retem bushes.

Joshua easily overlooked the breach of orders by the youth in behalf of his brother, and to his friend, Caleb, he observed that there would be good time, he hoped, to train the young in strict discipline and obedience, such as might befit the armies of the Lord.

Adoram was carried to his father's tent, there to be nursed by Zillah and his sisters, and all night resounded the wailings of poor Malbeth, which were re-echoed by Sherah,

Keren, and Axa, with others of the women. Though each had her own dearest safely at home again, it was due, in courtesy and sympathy, to assist in bemoaning a kinsman, in a song of lamentation, each verse of which ended in a metrical howl. Such piteous songs and cries reverberated all round the camp, wherever the men had rushed forth in their passionate self-will and folly, never to return. For the loss had really been terrible. Each prince missed a large proportion of his tribe, though the destruction seemed to have especially fallen on the 'mixed multitude' from Egypt, people of all nations, who had followed the Israelites to escape from rule, and had straggled out in search of plunder. But even to the most worldly wise it was plain that the tribes were in no condition to attempt the invasion of Palestine. Few had faith or courage enough to deserve to hope for supernatural help.

Adoram was penitent over his transgression as he lay upon his couch of skins and rugs, and was very anxious to atone for it before moving from Kadesh. As soon as he could leave the tent, he, accompanied by his father and brothers, led up a goat to the court of the Tabernacle, to be offered as a sin-offering in expiation of his fault. It was Eleazar, the son of Aaron, who received him, and heard his wish.

'Strictly speaking,' Eleazar said, 'the sin-offering is only permitted in cases of absolute ignorance. Wilful and gross sins can be atoned for by no present sacrifice.'

Adoram's face fell; Ulim interceded for him. 'I was not present. He did not hear me forbid him, and his zeal overpowered him.'

Eleazar said that he would go and consult Moses, and the father and all the brothers remained prostrate in earnest prayer in the court of the Tabernacle, until the priest appeared again.

The plea was accepted. Since Adoram was still a youth, and had erred more through haste and zealous enterprise than self-will, his

error might be treated as a sin of ignorance.

So he was permitted to stand at the door
of the Tabernacle, and lay his hand upon the
goat, confessing over it that he had sinned,
greatly sinned, against God and against his
father and mother, and entreating God to
look upon him and have mercy on him.

The goat was then slain by a brief rapid
blow, in token of the death deserved by sin.
Eleazar dipped his finger in the blood, and
sprinkled seven times towards the veil within ;
he touched the horns protruding from the
brazen altar of incense with the blood, and
the rest was poured into a pit before the
altar of burnt - offering prepared for it.
Levites extracted parts of the animal, which
were laid on the altar and burnt with incense,
and the remainder was carried away by them
to be burnt without the camp.

Adoram was but partially recovered, and
felt that the goat endured the death he had
merited, and that the vultures might even

now be flapping their wings over his bones. It was a painful atonement, grievous to witness, and he was faint and giddy with the sight and the fumes, so that his father had to hold him up, while Aaron who had now advanced from the sanctuary said : ' Peace be with thee, my son, peace in the name of the Lord God, who hath a better and fuller pardon in store for them that seek Him.   Go in peace, and pardon be with thee !'

CHAPTER XVIII

REBELLION

How long endure this priestly scorn,
Ye sons of Israel's eldest born ;
Shall two, the meanest of their tribe
To the Lord's host the way prescribe ?

KEBLE.

THERE was no further attack by the enemy,
before the cloud was lifted up and guided
the encampment, no more northward to the
Holy Land, but southward towards the
eastern gulf of the fork of the Red Sea, and
thence they moved into the great desert of
Paran, the northern division of the peninsula,
a tableland of rocky soil, tossed about like
stormy waves, but not devoid of water, nor
of pasture in the valley, though it was a
dreary exchange for their hopes of the land

flowing with milk and honey, which seemed doubly inviting after they had forfeited it till forty years' end.

And from Moses came forth that mournful hymn, known to us as the 90th Psalm, which was sung round the camp, by some like a dirge over their dead and their own shortened life, by others, such as Ulim and Sherah, in exultation over God's eternal power, and in hope for their children :

Show Thy servants Thy work,
And their children Thy glory ;
And the glorious majesty of the Lord be upon us.
Prosper thou the work of our hands upon us. O prosper
    Thou our handiwork.

But the bright hopes of the first year were a good deal depressed, and there were many widows besides Malbeth. She was a warm-hearted, affectionate woman, like wax in the hands of her husband ; and Adoram, who had always liked her, announced his intention of marrying her, so soon as the days of her mourning should be accomplished, and taking upon him the care of her two little boys.   She was older than he, had Egyptian blood, and moreover many Egyptian superstitions, and it was not the marriage Ulim and Zillah would have desired for him ; but Malbeth was a heavy care to them, and they pitied her, so Ulim blessed the wedlock, though there were no such rejoicings as for Mirglip and Dumah.

There were serious murmurs arising however when the encampment had been formed at Rimmon, where was a Midianite village ornamented with pomegranate trees from which it was named.   It was apparent that there was no intention of approaching the Land of Promise, and the Reubenites, never well affected to Moses, and whose tribe had suffered severely at Hormah, the place of destruction, began to complain loudly. There had always been an amount of jealousy among them of the leadership of Israel.

Jacob had evidently considered Joseph as his heir, as being the son of his chosen

wife, and Reuben, Simeon, and Levi had
been set aside from the precedence, Reuben
for his personal character and transgression,
the other two for their savage violence
towards the Shechemites; and Joseph first,
and then Judah, stood before them; Judah
being further distinguished by mysterious
prophecy.

But in this the sons of Reuben did not
acquiesce.   They remembered that their
forefather was the first-born of all the sons,
and resented the predominance of Moses;
and now that they found the course of the
Israelites turned back into the dismal hills
of Paran, instead of proceeding into the
Promised Land, their murmurings began to
take head.

Their encampment bordered on that of
the Kohathite Levites, and Korah had
become intimate with Dathan, the chief com-
plainer; though Korah, a more far-seeing
man, did not so much resent the delay in the
wilderness, as the exclusive rights of the

priesthood being restricted to Aaron and his sons. Sherah found him sitting in front of his own tent, arguing with Adoram and Dumah while Mirglip stood by, leaning against the tent-pole, and Keren as usual taking part with her brother.

'Have we not heard that all the congregation are holy, a royal priesthood, a peculiar people? Every one of us heard it, every one has Abraham for his father! Why should one family alone be singled out as worthy to offer incense?'

'As well say that none other might offer prayer or sing a hymn of praise,' added Keren.

'Yea, and are those chosen specially endowed?' continued Korah. 'We have seen how Aaron fell away to idols, for want of firmness. We have seen how Nadab and Abihu sinned.'

'And their punishment,' put in Mirglip.

'And what is Eleazar better than they? How did he escape but by being younger?

What is Phinehas save a mere warrior at heart? What have they done to have the preference above all?'

'They are chosen of God. Why ask further?' said Mirglip.

'So Moses says, but we heard no voice mark them out; we only have his word for it. I say not that he means to deceive, but a fasting man, in the midst of strange visions, might well think he heard what was only in his own soul.'

Upon this, Mirglip shouldered his shepherd's staff, held out his arm to Àxa, and walked away, only turning to say, 'Thou art elder than I, Korah. I lay my hand on my mouth, but I will not hear such blasphemy.'

Korah shrugged his shoulders. 'Good young Mirglip is simple,' he said; 'he believes all that he is told. But we are wiser men. It is time for us to make a stand and claim our rights, as of the royal priesthood. Let us fashion to ourselves censers, and claim our right of bearing incense to the altar.'

'I did not fare well when I followed counsel other than that of Moses,' said Adoram.

'Oh!' scoffed Korah, 'hast thou not forgotten the smart of the Amorite arrows?'

'No, no, no,' screamed Malbeth, throwing herself upon him. 'I will not have him led into peril by evil counsel.'

'Peril?' demanded Keren; 'what peril can there be? Why should we be deprived of ministering?—we, who have far more of the spirit of prophecy than ever belonged to Aaron and his sons, or indeed to Moses, who ever was noted for a slow tongue. Claim thy rights, brother, and all the congregation will stand by thee.'

'I shall claim not only mine, but those of other princes,' returned Korah. 'The eldest son was ever the priest of his father's house until now! Adoram, thou wilt come with me?'

'Nay, nay, nay, I beseech thee, my lord and husband,' cried Malbeth, rushing forward, and clinging to him. 'Have I not suffered enough through venturesomeness and disobedience? Have pity on me and my babes, whom thou didst promise to guard as thine own. What is it to thee who offers incense?'

She wept aloud, and between his recent experience, and his love and pity for her, besides his knowledge of his father's certain opinion, he was ready to reassure her, adding too that the Levites had been accepted instead of the eldest sons of other tribes, who had been redeemed, like Zuriel, Mirglip's child.

At that minute Dathan came marching up to the camp of the Ben Beriah. He was a tall, large, warlike man, clad in a large striped burnouse, gaudy with blue, brown, red, and white, from which his black eyes and bearded face looked out fiercely. He used a long spear as a staff, and might have been taken for an Amalekite chieftain. He was a contrast to Korah, who wore a white tunic bordered with blue, crossed with a white ephod, and a mantle of the same colour to shade his head from the sun.

'The spirit works,' he said to Korah, after exchanging greetings with the younger men; 'there are many who join with me in holding ourselves deceived by all these shows of miracles and divine voices. Nothing is plainer than that Moses' whole design is to lead us about in the desert till his power is fully established, then it may be to sell our swords to Egypt. Hast thou here any fresh supporters?'

'Where is thine uncle, Dumah?' anxiously asked Sherah.

'He is taking counsel with the elders in the tent of Moses,' said Dumah.

'Go and seek him, my son, unless Mirglip be already gone!'

But Dumah lingered, while Korah spoke. 'I deem not that to be his intention. It is rather to hold us back in Paran, while the Egyptians pass by on their war with the

Hittites. But it is the assuming to one small family in the tribe all the honours of the priesthood that angers me.'

'Priesthood and princedom, that is over much for one family, and that not among the chiefest in Israel, not even descended from the eldest son,' added Dathan. 'How doth Elishama bear with it, since Ephraim had pretensions to supremacy?'

'Elishama is an old man, his son Nun died in the flower of his days, and as to Oshea—or Joshua as it pleaseth Moses to call him—he is so much favoured and promoted that maybe he will set Gershom aside, and seize the foremost place for himself,' said Korah. 'Be it so; I heed not who is leader, so that Aaron's seed thrust us not aside from offering to the Maker and Lord of all.'

'True! oh true, my brother,' echoed Keren; 'all alike have power to approach to God. We need no pomp of priesthood between Him and ourselves, such as that wherewith they would set us afar off.'

'My daughter,' said Sherah, 'under-
standest thou not how that all may offer
prayer and praise, the fruit of their lips; yet
God is a King, and calls on us to approach
Him in His courts as a King with all
solemnity, through those whom He has
chosen?'

'That is the point,' said Korah. 'Whom
did He choose? Once it was the first-born.
Why are they set aside, with a strange
ceremony to account for it, save to gratify
the resolve of Moses and Aaron to reserve
to themselves the whole rights of the priestly
caste?'

The discussion was still going on when
Ulim approached, and announced that Moses
had heard of the complaints against him, and
called upon all the discontented to come up
to the gates before the Tabernacle and try
conclusions with him.

'Yea, so we will,' said Korah. 'It shall
be put to the proof who are the special
choice of the Lord, and worthy alone to

serve Him. Ulim, do thou come with me, and vindicate the right of heads of households to stand before the Lord.'

'A royal priesthood, by our covenant,' cried Keren. 'We will not forfeit our privilege, nor let all be absorbed by those sons of Levi, who take advantage of their nearer relation to Moses.'

'Alas!' said Ulim to Sherah, 'I greatly fear that these young men will bring judgment on themselves, though they think all is zeal for their right to worship the Lord.'

'It is to be feared,' said Sherah, 'that it is not half so much zeal for worship as jealousy of Aaron and Eleazar! And for Dumah, I specially fear and pray, his wife has so much influence over him.'

They were interrupted by Abiram, who was stalking proudly by, and calling out to Dathan, 'Come, brother, the people listen. Now is the time to make a stand! We will not come up at Moses' beck and call, as though he were the Great Prince over all

the camp. Show thyself a true sheikh!
Ulim, be not faint-hearted. Bring all the
gallant Ben Beriah!'

'Away, proud and rebellious men,' replied
Ulim. 'Tempt not my sons to defiance of
their God.'

There was a sneer of 'So Moses says.
Thou, a wise man, thus easily deceived!'

'No more of this,' insisted Ulim, raising
his staff. 'My sons obey me; and I forbid
them to follow those who rise against the
Lord who led us from Egypt, and gives us
daily food. Leave my tents, I command
you.'

Abiram laughed, and said something
about the tamarisk trees being plentiful; but
this was too absurd to need an answer, since
no tamarisk gum could account for the regular supply of manna nor for the Sabbath omis-
sion. Dathan called out rudely and defiantly to
the young men, 'We reckon upon you! You
will see to-morrow, and will stand with us.'

Korah only tarried to say a few words to

his sister, and the four ringleaders passed on, while Ulim clasped his hands, raised them to heaven, and exclaimed : 'O God, be merciful to us, and to this perverse generation.'

For, as he told Sherah, disaffection was widely spread among the congregation. The defeat at Hormah was forgotten, and the younger men, who had been recently acquiring some dexterity in the use of their weapons, fancied that nothing need restrain them from going on to conquer save Moses' timidity ; and that wandering in the desert would merely be dropping all the civilisation they had learnt in Egypt : while others were not unwilling to lead the wild nomadic life, only not under the strict regulations that Moses was constantly promulgating and enforcing ; and some would have given up all hope and returned to the ease and plenty of Egypt, forgetting all the slavery.

A very large proportion of the people dwelt on their grievances, and only had needed leaders to bring them to a head, and demand something definite ; and these had come forward in the three Reubenites and in Korah, who had a complaint of his own, in which he found many to participate. The political and religious systems established, not by Moses, but by God Himself at Mount Sinai, were both assailed, and a demonstration in force was preparing for the morrow.

Ulim told Sherah that he had been horrified to find the extent of the discontent and ingratitude that pervaded the camp, and the multitudes who were ready to rise if these determined leaders once began. He had no doubt that God would show His power, and win the victory ; but there was a heavy foreboding on the faithful man that it would be at the cost of heavy punishment on the faithless people—perhaps by letting the various parties rise and destroy one another.

Nor, alas ! could he be absolutely confident of the part the Ben Beriah would take, or even of all his own immediate family.

Adoram was sorely tempted, having seen the Land of Promise, and hungering after it; and Dumah hankered to follow Korah. His wife, eager to support her brother, was half the night preparing incense and seeking for a little censer which she had brought from Egypt. And, at the same time, Sherah in her part of the tent, Mirglip and Axa in theirs, were praying that he might not be led into presumptuous sin.

They heard not how Moses and Aaron, prostrate on the ground, were pleading for the perverse people. 'O God, the God of the spirits of all flesh, shall one man sin and wilt Thou be wroth with all the congregation?'

CHAPTER XIX

THE GAINSAYING OF KORAH

Thus spake the proud at prime of morn ;
Where was their place at eve ? Ye know :
Rocks of the wild in sunder torn,
And altars scath'd with fires of woe.

KEBLE.

THE camp was astir early in the morning as the light faded from shining over
the sanctuary to the paler pillar of cloud.
Sherah gazed eagerly to see whether there
were any portent there such as might
at least deter her son from joining in the
rash endeavour; but she only saw the rainbow flickering on it, and that, indeed, was
seldom visible to other eyes than hers.
Ulim went forth to join Elishama in case
Moses needed the support of the elders.

Adoram was withheld as much by his wife's entreaties to venture nothing perilous as by his father's command, Mirglip by his own strong sense of duty.   But Sherah, with tears in her eyes, saw Dumah set forth, actually led by Keren, who bore the censer in her hand, while her eyes shone with a strange lustre as she chanted—

> ' And shall we not come near,
>   We who are Abraham's seed,
>   Come near to offer to our Lord ? '

They disappeared among the tents. Sherah, 'Zillah, and the rest fell on their knees, or prostrate on the ground.   Suddenly there was a shriek of terror—a light that glared through the hands and through the eyelids.   The pillar was flashing forth lightnings above.

'Oh! my son! my son!' wailed Sherah. But in another second Dumah and Keren, hand in hand, flying as from an avenger, came rushing headlong through the avenue of tents.   Dumah hid his face—he was a

mere boy—in his mother's robe. Keren
stood still, wringing her hands, and wailing :

'My brother! oh, my brother!'

'The fire!—the lightning!' sobbed Dumah;
—'is it coming?'

And at that moment there was a strange
rumbling and quaking : the earth beneath
them shook, and a horrible cry came up from
the Reubenite camp, re-echoed from the
Kohathite tents, and back from all the host,
breaking out again and again as the trembling continued ; and the tents shook, some
falling flat down, others fairly collapsing
under the pressure of crowds of the Reubenites, who came, mad with terror, rushing
wildly in upon the Ephraimites, screaming,
shrieking, trampling on one another.

Then Ulim's voice was heard calling on
his sons and the others of the Ben Beriah
to support Elishama and Joshua in withstanding the frenzied shock, and the earthquake being apparently over, it was possible
to obtain a certain calm. But there was a

terrible sense of awe and horror over all the
congregation, and only gradually were Ulim
and Dumah able to speak, and give an
account of what they had seen.

Dumah had reached the enclosure round
the Tabernacle, where the other aspirants to
the priesthood, two hundred and fifty in
number, were gathered, each bearing a
censer.   Keren still carried his, and tried to
thrust it on him; but there was something
in the aspect of the light above the Holy of
Holies which made him hang back, and feel
that such an offering would not be acceptable.
Thus it was that what Moses said he did not
hear; but he was not among the body of men
who pressed rudely forward, censer in hand,
to present their incense.   He only saw the
flashing forth of the light of glory, trans-
formed into a lightning flame and shock,
before which every man was falling—all the
two hundred and fifty in ghastly heaps.   All
that he and Keren could do was to fly headlong back, not knowing whether the scathing

bolt was on them or not, even when they fell down breathless and panting on the ground at their own tents.

There they sat, trembling still and shuddering the more, as Ulim told of Dathan, Abiram, and On having refused to obey the summons of Moses, and gathered together their partisans round their tents. Moses, attended by Elishama and most of the other elders, had gone forth in solemn, unarmed procession—a contrast to the troop of rebels whom they found drawn up in front of their tents, armed to the teeth with spears, javelins, swords, and daggers—the very boys carrying bows and arrows. They met Moses with shrieks of defiance and fierce demands: 'Where is thy promised land?' and the weapons were levelled at him, as he stood still, calm, before them, calling out to the people who pressed round to depart from the tents of these wicked men lest they too should be consumed. The solemn warning had its effect; there was a press backwards of many of the rebels, but still the four chiefs stood in their tent doors, with their families around them, in defiance of the grave, mournful, judicial form before them.   Aloud he called on Israel to behold.   'If these men die the common death of all men, or if they be visited after the visitation of all men, then the Lord hath not sent me!   But if the Lord make a new thing, and the earth open her mouth and swallow them up with all that appertain to them, and they go down alive into the grave, then ye shall understand that these men have provoked the Lord.'

Even as he spoke a huge fissure opened in the ground; tents, men, women, and children—all sank into it, with cries of utter horror and despair, which were lost as, with another shock, the earth closed in once more, and all were gone!   Gone!   Whither?   Into an abyss that closed on them while yet alive, while their shrieks yet echoed in the ears of the congregation.

Such was the fearful history that Ulim

uttered, still pale with awe, and shuddering as he spoke, while Keren clung to her husband as though uncertain whether he were safe or not.

The earthquake had ceased, and she implored him to take her to the tent of her mother and of Korah's wife, that she might know how it fared with them, and ascertain his fate.

For she had not seen him among the two hundred and fifty would-be priests ; nor could Ulim be certain whether he had been with Dathan and the rest. Her strong affection gave her vigour enough in spite of the shock of dismay at what she had seen, felt, and heard ; and with her head wrapped in her veil, she even walked faster than Dumah on her way to the Kohathite encampment, passing by the space in front of the Reubenites which no one dared to occupy or even own. The Reubenites seemed to be all huddled together in shrinking terror in the distance.

Q

Looking across towards the Tabernacle, in the court were seen Levites moving about, removing the remains of those who had perished.

'Ask, ask,' sobbed Keren to her husband, 'if *he* is there.'

Wrapped still more closely in her veil, she crouched on the outside of the canvas enclosure, while Dumah went forward with the mournful inquiry to one of the Levites whom he knew, but no satisfaction was to be had. Every face had been so scathed and burnt that recognition was impossible, especially as all had put on the white robes, and what was left of their dress was alike in all.

The Kohathite tents were untouched, except that a few of the nearest to the Reubenite had been thrown down by the shock, and Korah's was far advanced towards the Tabernacle. But his elder children were crying outside, no one near them. 'Father had never come back,' said the little boy Asaph, 'and mother was very sick.'

No! father had never come home, nor was it ever known whether he had died by the flame or perished in the earthquake. Keren and the rest of the family never could tell, though it is quite certain that he was destroyed, either with the two hundred and fifty who offered incense, or with Dathan and Abiram.

Keren, entering the tent, found nothing there but desolation. The poor young wife lay dying from the effects of the shock or alarm, and the assurance, which each moment confirmed, that the judgment had fallen on her husband. The stepmother had been struck by a falling pole, and lay dead on the ground. Poor Keren, she had hardly a moment to turn and look at the fallen figure, for the young wife was showing her the wailing infant, and gasping out, 'Love *his* children. Guard them, Keren, in the name of the Lord! Korah loved Him, though he would worship in his own way!'

The other Kohathite women were keeping

aloof in fright and repulsion, and Keren found herself alone with the dying woman, the two elder children, boys, Asaph and Zerah, and the infant Egla. All she could do was to ask Dumah to entreat his mother to come to her help, and to take the two children back with him.

They readily went with him, and ere his return the poor young wife had breathed her last. With him came his mother, sister, Zillah, and Malbeth. For Sherah, in so urgent a cause of compassion, braved the legal liabilities of uncleanness, as well as the terrors that hung about that region of the encampment, and came to the assistance of her daughter-in-law Keren, and the kind-hearted Malbeth, with showers of tears, and loud wailing, came and quite contended with Axa as to which should take the poor orphan babe to her bosom.

Nor was any blame attached to this tenderness to Korah's family, though he had died leading the defiance of Moses, and through him of the God who inspired Moses and chose Aaron. If Dathan had sinned through worldly ambition, and involved his relations in his fall, the error of Korah had come through presuming on his natural gifts of poetry and music ; and as he had not, like the Reubenites, disobeyed the summons of Moses, his young children had not been involved in the same catastrophe. Dumah made no objection to Keren's taking them to her tent, and her own marriage being childless, they were beloved and cherished like her own, indeed perhaps even more, for her love for her brother had been vehement, and full of an eager pride in his talent, and as she believed, his holiness, and as she truly said, in her first grief, she went mourning for him all her days.

CHAPTER XX

But must they die ? Will He, their Guardian Power,
Forsake them in affliction's darkest hour ?
No ! He the prayer hath heard : at His command
The mighty leader lifts His sovereign wand.

'ALAS!' said Ulim, 'even the terrible judgment has not warned our blind people. There are those among them who will not be persuaded that Moses does not deal with magic arts, and that it was he who produced the gulf that swallowed those unhappy men!'

'Utterly impossible,' cried Adoram. 'Was ever such a thing heard of, as that man should control an earthquake ?'

'Know precisely the time, and who should be swallowed?' added Mirglip.

'Even so, my son. If anything could

have convinced these murmurers in whose power Moses speaks and does his mighty works, it would be that which we have seen and heard.

'Also of the effect of withstanding God,' added Dumah.

'It is God's battle, not that of Moses,' said Ulim. 'So I have been telling the men of Reuben and of Gad, but they have, as it seems, been mingling with the men of the tribe of Jaakan, who hold Moses as a mighty enchanter, who caused the plagues of Egypt and the fires of Sinai, and they have persuaded the more daring to go forth and call Moses to account for causing the earthquake in which these, our unhappy brethren, perished.'

'Alas! alas!' said Mirglip, 'that we should further provoke our God.'

'Well mayest thou lament,' agreed Ulim. 'Our God is longsuffering, but will He suffer this?'

'Hearken!' exclaimed Mirglip. For

there was a general sound of shouting, a rattling as of weapons, and by climbing on a slight elevation, the brother could discern that a mass of men were advancing upon the cleared space before the Tabernacle, where judgment was wont to be given.

'Down, down on our knees,' cried Ulim. 'Let us pray that the presumption be not visited on them nor on us all.'

'Shall we not go to Moses' support?' demanded Adoram, while Mirglip clasped his weapon.

'Let us come, my sons, at least so far as the tents of Elishama, where we shall see whether we are to go forth in a body to warfare in the cause of the Lord! Daughters, entreat for us.'

Ulim and his sons went forth while the women knelt, or bowed themselves to the earth in trembling prayer that God would not desert His perverse and obstinate people.

Before long Ulim and his sons met a young lad, a messenger from Elishama and

Joshua, sent to summon them to the Tabernacle, but they found it very difficult to make their way through the dense throng of people.

Some cried out, 'Ah! you are convinced at last, ye sons of Ephraim! Ye go with us to show that we will no longer be led about blindfold by the magic arts that have cut off our brave men.'

'Blasphemer!' returned Ulim, 'dost not know that the Lord alone can cleave the solid earth?'

'Ah! ha! He is on the side of the oppressor! Down with him, the traitor to Israel,' and the men stooped for stones to cast at him.

Mirglip and Dumah had some difficulty in warding them off, while Adoram helped to force a way through the infuriated crowd. Presently another party thronged about them, Ephraimites this time.

'Back, Ulim, take not part with the deceivers who would put us under a worse tyranny than Pharaoh's.'

'He never slew the people and called it
his God's doing,' cried another voice.

'Shame on you, Huppim, and ye recreant Ephraimites, who have seen the fire
of God, who live on His bread from
heaven,' cried Ulim.

'Ha! ha! We know better than to be
gulled by Moses' tricks,' said the first.

'Come, Ulim, thou art an honoured man,
and we would spare thee. Back and share
not the doom of the misleaders of Israel.'

Ulim thrust the speaker aside, and
reached the space between the Levite tents,
where, among those of the Kohathites, his
wife and sister were performing the funeral
rites over the corpses of the mother and wife
of Korah.

The opening railed in around the courts
of the Tabernacle was before them, the place
where Moses and the elders sat in judgment. They gained it, and saw Moses, rod
in hand, standing on the elevated bank that
formed his tribunal, surrounded by a certain

proportion of the elders, Elishama among
them, and before him stood three or four
armed men, evidently haranguing him with
menacing gestures; and behind there was
gradually arising the frightful thunderous
growl of a multitude enraged, preparing to
burst in, and by their pressure sweep down
resistance before them. Comparatively only
a few — Levites under Phinehas, warriors
under Joshua—stood about the bank where
Moses towered with Aaron. A javelin
was even being pointed towards him as
Ulim and his sons pressed forward, hoping
to withstand the overwhelming rush that
was already breaking the bounds. Moses
uplifted his rod; therewith the glory flashed
out over the sanctuary !

Would the multitude still press on ?
Ay ! they did ! though the brightness,
beyond even that of lightning, shone in red
anger upon all around. All the elders and
the loyal fell on their faces, hiding their
eyes with hands and mantles, but even

through these they saw the terrible avenging
light; and yet they heard the crushing,
crashing sound continue as though the bounds
were giving way under the onward impulse
of the foremost ranks, driven on perhaps by
those behind. Another moment, and Ulim
and his sons expected to be trampled down
by the feet of hundreds and thus to suffer
with the whole congregation for the general
crime. The father muttered a groan of
'Mercy, good Lord!' but at the moment
the shouts of rage turned into howls of
anguish, 'exceeding bitter cries,' apparently
from all around, for they re-echoed from the
rear. Mirglip lifted his head for an instant,
and saw the front aggressors fallen dead, but
others, driven on by the uncontrollable impulse from behind, falling, writhing over
them in heaps, even as swarms of locusts
perish over the bodies of those slain by fires
in their flight.

As he hid his dazzled glance again, he
heard the voice of Moses, whose life even

now had been threatened. But it was not in anger or denunciation. No! It was in consternation, yet remedial, calling out to Aaron, 'Take a censer and put fire therein from off the altar, and put on incense, and go quickly unto the congregation and make an atonement for them; for there is wrath gone out from the Lord, the plague is begun.'

There was an interval, broken only by shrieks of pain and horror, but becoming more distant, then a sound as of some one passing by, and when Mirglip looked forth again, at the tinkling of golden bells and the sweet smell of incense, it was to see in the somewhat mitigated light, but veiled by the smoke of the incense that he bore, Aaron in full High Priest's garments hurrying forth at the head of attendant priests to stand between the dead and the living, and make atonement, that the stroke might be stayed.

Hiding his face again, he joined in his

father's whispered entreaty that the pleading of the High Priest might be accepted, that mystic intercession, betokening and anticipating that which was yet to come, of the Great High Priest offering His own Atonement, not for Israel alone but for all the sinful world. Silence ensued, and the soft sound of the bells was heard coming nearer. Father and sons ventured to move, the red wrathful light being now quenched into the ordinary brightness. A field of corpses lay before them, but Aaron was returning, and Moses coming from the altar of burnt-offering to meet him.

As Ulim and his sons knelt, feeling themselves to be alive and safe, Moses touched their brows, saying: 'Blessed be ye of the Lord, His faithful servants.'

A blessing from the great lawgiver in person was an honour that warmed the heart; but there was still anxiety for the fate of the wives, none knowing how far the judicial blast, or mysterious disease, had extended

before it was checked in mercy to Moses'
intercession and Aaron's atonement. The
corpses, already blackening, lay around, and
orders were given to heap sand over them,
while the alarm trumpets were blown, and
preparations put in hand for removing hastily
from the scene of presumption and of
judgment.

Ulim and Dumah found the tent that had
been Korah's deserted. The Kohathite
Levites around told them that the wife and
mother had been carried forth at night to be
buried, and that Sherah, Zillah, and Keren
had returned to their own abodes in early
dawn.

The father and son-in-law crossed the
camp, skirting past the region of death and
desolation, but meeting the upturned con-
vulsed face of him who had defied Ulim not
two hours previously. Arriving at their own
tribe, they found it for the most part untouched, and the Ben Beriah quite safe.
Adoram and Mirglip were already there,

and had relieved the anxiety of the women, who had suffered great terror from the reports of the insurrection at first; then from the manifestation of wrath, and the punishment which seemed to overwhelm all alike. Pale and awe-stricken, Zillah clung to her husband, though she said Sherah had all along declared that no harm could befall Ulim and Mirglip, for God would not destroy the righteous with the wicked.

Keren was still like one stunned, and seemed unable to think about anything save Zerah and Asaph, the two elder children of Korah. She held them, one in each arm, as she knelt, but seemed as if she would not heed if destruction overwhelmed them all together. Axa had charge of the little one, for Keren had rather hurt warm-hearted Malbeth's feelings by showing her desire that the Levite babe should be in the hands of none save a true Israelite.

Her ambition and jealousy were quelled.

She scarcely heeded when, after the removal of the camp from Rimmon, now so sadly marked, Aaron's divinely-appointed priest-hood was fully established by the wonder of his blossoming staff.

PART II

CHAPTER I

NEAR HOME

Here in the body pent,
  Absent from Him I roam,
Yet nightly pitch my moving tent,
  A day's march nearer home.
                    MONTGOMERY.

THE bustle of encampment was going on. All
was well organised, and each tribe, each clan,
each family knew their place by long custom ;
but still there could not but be much to be
done in taking down and unpacking the
tents from the waggons drawn by the oxen,
unrolling the mats and carpets carried thus
or by the asses, bringing out the cooking
vessels and other stores. Some of the
younger men and boys went to seek water
and others to watch the cattle and keep them

from encroaching or being encroached upon by the herds of other tribes. The younger women were attending to the arrangements of the tents, or superintending the children who were picking up dry retem boughs and lumps of old camels' dung to serve as fuel for cooking the evening meal. The very youngest were playing or rolling about on the sand under the watchful eyes of great-grandmother and grandmother, both with the early-aged features of eastern, sun-tanned women, but both vigorous still, though Sherah's hair was white as snow, and Axa's fast blanching. Still beauty could be traced in the calm expression of the mother, and the sweet sympathetic face of the daughter, as she comforted the child who had scratched his hand with a thorn.

'Mother,' said she, looking upward, 'surely we have been here before. It seems to me that I know the ragged peak of yonder mountain.'

'Surely, my daughter. That is the Mount of the Amorites, where presumptuous Israel was defeated by the enemy.'

' Then those must be the springs of Kadesh whither the maidens are gone ; as poor Keren and I used to go of old, with my little Zuriel on my back ! He who is now a stout warrior and thy brave father, my wondering little Belah ! ' she explained to the child.

' And didst thou not mark how we came through the cairns which marked the graves of those who died by the surfeit of the quails?' said Sherah.

' This is our old ground, a place of warning and of judgment,' said Axa, ' where—as I never shall forget—our men came streaming from the mountain-side, flying from their foes, where Adoram was scarcely saved, and Hatapha was slain.'

' And we turned back from the gates of the Land of Promise,' said Sherah.

' That was long ago ; Zuriel was a little babe, he is now a stalwart warrior ! Oh, mother, it must be well-nigh forty years since the sentence went forth.'

' Count, my daughter,' said Sherah, producing a little bag. 'I have dropped into this bag a red pebble every passover tide since we quitted Mount Sinai.'

The pebbles were spread on the mat, and Axa, numbering them, while the little Belah and Huldah were detained from appropriating them, exclaimed ' Thirty-seven, mother! Oh, can our wanderings be so nearly at an end and the land be before us?'

Sherah lifted up her eyes towards the hill below which the pillar of cloud had taken up a station above the ark. 'Who can tell, my child, what may be God's will for us? All we know is that His promise is certain ; but how quickly or what may go before, we know not, nor whether we shall see the land, or only these little ones reach it.

'The land, the land!' cried little Huldah. 'Oh, grandmother, tell us of the land where we shall see corn growing green.'

'And get sweet honey out of the rock,' echoed her brother Belah.

The children had been born in the wilder-

ness to parents who had known no other
home than a tent, no daily supply of food
save the manna, no leader but Moses, but
still with the hopes of Canaan held out before
them. So far as we know, these thirty-seven
years had passed without further incidents
than those of ordinary family life.   The
terrible judgments of Kadesh - Barnea and
Rimmon had not only destroyed most of the
disaffected and hopelessly rebellious Israelites,
too abject in spirit after their long slavery to
take heart for valiant efforts, though still able
to murmur and rebel, but they had trained
and subdued the minds of the survivors to
obedience to their leader and lawgiver.   A
hardy race, who had never known bondage,
had grown up in the desert life, and had been
carefully trained by the princes and elders in
all the warlike exercises then known.   The
younger ones had never even seen the idols
of Egypt, and though some, on the outskirts,
especially in the tribe of Simeon, had been
tainted by the idolatrous practices of the

neighbouring desert tribes, and had even been detected in setting up a tabernacle or chapel tent in honour of the Star Moloch or King Saturn or Time, devouring his offspring, yet the main body had been bred up in no worship save that of the Lord God Jehovah, and in the practice of the solemnities enjoined on Mount Sinai.

They were thus, with a few exceptions, a far more hopeful, resolute, and disciplined nation than that which had started from Egypt, and were composed in great part of middle-aged and youthful men, in the fulness of their strength, and trained to obey Joshua and Phinehas.

Meantime Ramses III., one of the ablest kings of Egypt, commonly known to his people as the Hornet, had passed by the direct route into Palestine, and there had fought with and conquered the Hittite and Hivite petty kingdoms, retreating afterwards to his own country, but leaving them with broken forces not able effectually to withstand the advance of the fresh invasion preparing in the peninsula of Paran.

Among the Ben Beriah things had gone well on the whole, under the wise influence of Ulim and Sherah, the latter of whom had begun to be looked on almost in the light of a prophetess among her people.

Axa and Mirglip had gone on their quiet way, and Mirglip was an active elder in his father's old age, his eldest son, Zuriel, leader of a division of the host. Zuriel had married Egla, the daughter of Korah, one of the children so tenderly and anxiously brought up by Keren.

Poor Keren seemed to have no thought or care for anything else after the loss of her brother. Her eager aspirations were all over, and she devoted herself to the care of the little orphans, especially to training the boys Zerah and Asaph to the tasks of a Kohathite, leading them daily to watch the sacrifice and teaching them to sing. She hardly attended to her duties towards Dumah, and he justly complained that he had no wife in her. After a few years, it ended in his bringing home another young wife from Judah, called Helah. Sherah was grieved, for it was held better to have only one wife, but there was no law against it, so that she could not object ; but Helah despised the childless Keren, and held her to be under a curse, as sister to Korah, and the children as blighted by their father's doom, so that Dumah only obtained peace by procuring another tent where Keren could abide with the three. She had grown very meek, all her self-assertion had ceased, and she only exerted herself to defend the children. She lived till Egla was wedded to Zuriel, and Asaph, like his brother, had been admitted among the Levites, then she sank and died peacefully in Sherah's arms, only begging to be buried as near as possible to the cave where the two hundred and fifty had been laid. The distance was not too great, and Dumah, Mirglip, and the two young Levites complied with the request, though Helah

sneered at her desire to lie near to one
doomed by God Himself. Zillah, wife to
Ulim, and tender-hearted Malbeth had also
died, but Hatapha's sons still kept with the
Ben Beriah, middle-aged men by this time, but
showing something of the Egyptian in their
tastes and ways. Adoram had sons of his
own, and so had the youngest of Ulim's sons,
Zemira, as well as the daughters. In fact
the numbers of all the families of Israel had
multiplied exceedingly in the wilderness, nor
did age or decrepitude come on the elders in
the healthy life that they were leading. The
supply of manna was unfailing, and seemed
to afford vigour to those who partook chiefly
of this, and did not hanker after the occasional
food that they derived from other quarters.
It was observable, too, that they never became
footsore, however continual their journeys,
and that their garments remained fresh and
good in spite of sunshine and occasional
tempests of rain and sand. The thoughtful,
like Sherah and Axa, felt that they were in a

supernatural condition, strangely guarded and guided, but the younger people took all as a matter of course, and hardly understood them when they told of the toils of Egypt, or of daily life in a settled country.

The preparations for the halt were just completed, and the young wives were coming in with pitchers only half filled when Ulim was seen approaching, leaning indeed on a staff, but still a noble figure with his white beard and venerable deportment, and attended by Mirglip and Zemira.

The great-grandchildren ran out to meet him, and he laid his hands in blessing on them as they came up. 'Children,' he said, 'under God's guidance, ere long will ye be inheriting the great promise!'

'Then, father,' said Axa, 'we are verily about to win the glorious home.'

'The home we hoped for in our sore bondage,' exclaimed Sherah, clasping her hands and looking upwards, 'the home of Abraham, and where Joseph our father is to rest,' she added, looking towards the tent where the embalmed corpse of Joseph was enshrined.

'Yea,' said Ulim, gravely, 'but there is much to come ere we are at rest. Our youth have grown up in peaceful days, but they will be called on in their turn to acquit themselves like men, and be strong, and our women to be patient.'

'Father, father, there is hardly any water,' was a cry that came up from Egla and the rest of the young women.

'It is scant and muddy,' added Helah, 'and the men of the Reubenites drove us away, though we told them thou wert a great sheikh in Israel.'

'Ah, daughter, I told thee thou wouldst have to be patient. We have heard that cry before, sister,' he added to Sherah.

'And the Lord answered it,' she said.

'He will answer it in His mercy, doubt not of it,' said the old man. 'Only murmur not against Him, my children, and be patient and sparing of what we have. Mirglip and two more from other tribes are to be sent on the morrow to Selah to ask of the nation of Edom a passage through their mountains, seeing that they are our brethren, and if they grant it, all will go well with us, as far as the borders of Moab.'

'Oh!' cried Egla, 'this is what my mother Keren taught us to long for. I mind me of the song she taught us.' And she turned away chanting—

'The people shall hear and be afraid;
Pangs have taken hold of the inhabitants of Philistia,
Then the Sheikhs of Edom are amazed,
The mighty men of Moab, trembling hath taken hold of them;
All the inhabitants of Canaan have melted away.'

'Miriam's song!' said Sherah. 'How fresh and hopefully we sang it on the shore of the Red Sea, little guessing the weary years that were to come after it.'

'By our own sin,' responded Ulim, 'because of the faintness of heart that turned back! And alas! Sherah, Miriam the prophetess is one who will not sing her song in the land of rest.'

'She is dying then, as we feared.'

'Even so; she was scarcely living when they halted beneath a shittim tree for shade, and she will scarce see morning light. Never did I see Moses so grieved and bowed down as by thus losing the sister who watched him as a babe and loved him through all.

'Yet she had her errors,' said Axa; 'she spoke against him once.'

'She suffered and repented,' said Ulim. 'Ah! it is not for absence of faults that we are beloved, for who is he that sinneth not? But Moses and Aaron had ever hoped that those three, so marvellous in their strength and youthfulness, would be spared to lie down and find their rest in the land of promise.'

'She finds her rest elsewhere,' said Sherah.

'As well he knows, but the parting after their long life together cannot but make him

S

sore-hearted. I would fain spare him a fresh outcry of these impatient people. We will send the young men out to seek for wells in the hills around.'

'Ah!' said Sherah, 'partings and sorrows come closer the nearer we are to home, whether our rest be first in the Land or in that further Land.'

'As it is like to be with me,' said Ulim. 'Nay, start not, sister, I was not exempted from the doom as were the Levites and Caleb and Joshua. Elishama is gone, and —nay, children, I feel no sickness—but I am content to wait my call, for I know I am to be redeemed from another yoke than Egypt's.'

CHAPTER II

Moses, the man of meekest heart,
  Lost Canaan by self-will,
To shew, when Grace has done its part
  How sin defiles us still.

                              J. H. NEWMAN.

ULIM's wish for Moses was not fulfilled. The quest for water was not successful, through all the arid district of Kadesh, though it was carried on through the days of mourning for Miriam, and murmurs loud and deep, such as those which had 'tempted God' in Massah, began to wax more and more, while the camp waited to hear the result of the embassy to Edom.

Ulim was uneasy, not only at the re-currence of the old riotous murmurs to

which in former years he had been so
well accustomed, and which Enhat repeated
almost in the words of his father Hatapha,
but at their effect upon Moses. Whether
it was from having been long without direct
revelation, or from his long exercise of
authority, or from the prospect of being a
great conqueror, and recalling the campaigns
of his youth in Egypt, Moses was certainly
less patient of contradiction, less apt to refer
to the Supreme Guidance, and more arbitrary,
and this mood was enhanced by the grief and
soreness of heart induced by his recent bereavement of a beloved sister.

The people had come together before the
Tabernacle, and there was that angry buzzing
murmur like swarming bees, growing into
muttering thunder, too evident a recurrence
to the ways of the forefathers long ago at
Massah, while the spokesman of the tribes
spoke harshly and bitterly of the disappointment of finding themselves in no place of
seed or of pomegranates. Were they to

perish here? Would they had died with their fathers!'

Again the light on the sanctuary shone out, Moses and Aaron retired within the Holy Place, while the people waited in awe and a certain alarm till they came forth again, Moses bearing like a sceptre the mystic rod with its blossoms, holding his head high aloft, and with a countenance that had as much indignant displeasure as authority in it.

He led the way to a lofty cliff which shut in the valley where they were encamped, and his words were stern, arrogating as it were to himself the power of the miracle.

'Will water come?' thought Ulim; 'neither he nor Aaron looks as he did at Massah. Does God let His power be shown when man is wroth? Yet it is just wrath, for these people are perverse and faithless!'

He clasped his son's arm close in his anxiety as Moses' voice rang out, clear and powerful, as, standing with Aaron, he exclaimed, 'Hear now, ye rebels, must we fetch water out of this rock?'—then struck upon the marble face with the rod.

No water followed!

Ulim hid his face on Zemira's shoulder in consternation, but his son cried out joyfully. The stroke had been repeated, a hasty sharp stroke, the stream burst forth abundantly, while a shout of acclamation followed from all the multitude. Moses' supremacy was again established over the younger generation as over the elder, and as he turned away the impulsive people were kneeling to drink of the limpid pure water as it rushed along, then throwing themselves before him to kiss his garments and owning him, some with loud cries, others with sobs of gratitude, as the protector and saviour who would lead them to possess the Land.

Never had Moses seemed to have a greater triumph. Those young people, with whom the past wonders had been matters of hearsay and tradition, perhaps only partly credited, or thought to be at an end, crowded round waving their arms, and crying out, 'Thou art our benefactor and wonder-worker, who hast led us out of Egypt. Thou shalt lead us to conquer the land. We will follow thee to victory. No fears nor doubts while Moses and Aaron are at our head.'

Once the two brothers marched along, grand, benign, dignified figures, Moses with his snowy beard flowing over his white garments, Aaron in his priestly vestments, the golden mitre and the jewelled breast-plate glittering in the sunbeams. Their age rendered them the more dignified, but did not impair their noble and erect bearing, nor the firm activity of their steps. Behind them came in solemn procession Eleazar, Phinehas, and the other priests ; also Joshua and a band of chosen warriors, and all burst out into a song of joy and victory.

'It is strange,' said Ulim as he stood listening ; 'I do not hear praise of the Lord God, but chiefly of Moses.'

'No doubt such will be rendered in the Holy Place, apart from this tumultuous youth,' said Sherah.

Keren had trained her nephews to be adroit scribes, as became Levites, and Zerah was sure to be called upon to record the wonder of the Rock of Kadesh. Still, though received among the Kohathites, he clung to the house of the Ben Beriah, having married Azubah, the daughter of Mirglip, and he used to come to read to Ulim and Mirglip the sentences that he had written out.

Alas! on this day it was no triumphant note. He came with dejected face and sat down before Ulim on the ground, waiting to be asked by his elders what was his grief. 'Was it an evil answer from Edom?' he was asked.

'Alas! no, my father; then would we not fear. But God's sentence hath been spoken, and on our leader, our great leader himself.'

'Not smitten and taken from us?' cried Axa, ready to rend her garments and tear her hair if so it proved.

'No, he is not taken from us as yet, but the sentence hath gone forth.   It seems that the word of God to him was that he should bear the rod, and speak to the rock, not smite it.'

'Ah!' said Ulim; 'so would it have been proved that, not in his own power, nor in any magic virtue of the rod, were the marvels wrought.'

Zerah bowed his head in assent, adding, 'I know not how it was, whether in anger at the dull perverseness of the tribes, renewing the ways of their fathers of old, or from the habit of giving commands as from himself, but he forgot and transgressed the command to speak instead of striking.'

'Alas!' said Ulim, as his misgivings were verified.

'And this is the word of God that came to him, and which, as a scribe, he bade me write:

" Because ye believed Me not, to sanctify Me in the eyes of the children of Israel, therefore ye shall not bring this congregation into the land which I have given them." '

Ulim bowed to the ground in mingled reverence, submission, and grief. He began to understand. He understood more as he thought it over, and as he spake later with Moses himself, under sentence indeed, but not in wrath.

The temper that had for all these years been used to command had acquired a tone that was impatient and arbitrary, and the old habits of a leader in the Egyptian life had returned. To become the conqueror of Palestine would only have fostered the spirit ; dealing with the subdued nations for death or slavery, and portioning out the inheritance of the tribes, might have been a trial that would have been too great for his character, and therefore, as far as human judgment can understand, he was spared it, so that he

VIEW FROM MOUNT HOR

might still continue the greatest, the holiest,
the nearest to God.

There were still tasks for him to fulfil, and
a year still he spent with a subdued spirit,
changed from the hopeful confidence that
was almost becoming presumption, and Ulim
and Sherah grieved for him in their tents.

The mourning was deepened when the
camp had moved on eastward for a day's
journey up a broad valley to the foot of a
remarkable mountain, known to them as Hor
or Moserah, looking, with its tall cliffs and
peaks, like a citadel. Several routes branched
from it up the different wadys or valleys.
Here the return of the messengers was
awaited, and here the sentence began to be
in part fulfilled. Aaron, attended by Moses
and Eleazar, was to go up into the mountain
and die. Fully robed, walking as well
as usual, while the Levites chanted a dirge
and the people wept and wailed, he ascended
the rugged path, the people watching the
three figures till they were hidden by the

rocks.   Moses and Eleazar came down without him.   He lay in the cave of the mountain where they placed him reverently. Eleazar returned in the sacred robes.   And thus was prefigured the High Priest for ever.

CHAPTER III

A better covenant, disciplined
From shadowy types to truth, from flesh to spirit.
MILTON.

FOR thirty days the camp remained beneath the lofty cliffs of Mount Hor, mourning for Aaron, while Moses secluded himself in grief, repentance, and humiliation. The tribes were also waiting for the return of the messengers sent to demand a passage through the hills of Edom by the regular caravan route, which, as could already be seen, led between the purple porphyry cliffs through an open winding valley.

Mirglip and the rest came back saying that they had travelled easily up the valley, finding that below the purple and crimson peaks were lower hills of chalk, with rich gorges between them, clothed with bright verdure, trees and flowers, refreshing to their eyes.   And thus they came to Selah (the Rock, Petra in later days), a strange red city of caves hollowed in the sandstone cliffs, which nearly closed in overhead.   Partly by Nature, partly by art, these 'nests in the rock' had been made and the openings of the larger ones had been carved out ornamentally. In one of these, fitted up with rich hangings from Egypt or from Phœnicia, or both, the king of Edom received the messengers, but he was not at all favourable to them.   He sat, with an Egyptian crown on his head, a purple embroidered robe round him, and a spear as a sceptre in his hand, which he evidently longed to throw at them, and he treated them as if they were nothing but wild Ishmaelites from the desert, as perhaps they looked ; he scoffed at their claim to brotherhood, through Esau of old, and as to the promise to keep to the highway, through which Egypt and Tyre traded, he laughed at it, as a mere pretence for invading his land.   He did the embassy no harm, according to the honour of the country, as they had eaten salt with his people, but he warned them to hasten away, and not to meddle with invading his mountains.

Indeed, before Mirglip and the rest had regained Moserah, they had seen the caves bristling with warriors, javelins and bows in hand, and heaps of stones ready to be rolled down on them.   Passage in that direction was impossible, without miraculous help, and this was not to be expected, as it was to be remembered that Edom, however churlish, was the brother of Israel, nor had yet broken entirely away from the God of Abraham.

Indeed Mirglip had heard in the evenings round the camp fire fragments of a wonderful poem on the trials of an ancient Edomite, and of the vindication of God's ways with man, although they may often be hard to understand and as far out of reach as the wonders of the ostrich, the battle-horse, the crocodile, or the stars.

At any rate the path through Edom was not to be forced, and, much dispirited, the Israelites had to turn back southwards, so as to reach the Gulf of Akabah, and go up on the east or wilderness side of Edom. Nor did they avoid a battle, for the Canaanites came out and fell on the stragglers, in the very spot where the battle had been fought thirty-eight years previously, but with very different effect, for the Canaanites were utterly routed, and Hormah, or 'utter destruction,' pertained to them instead of to the Israelites.

In spite of this success there was much depression. Not only was the journey backward instead of forward, but the ground was horribly trying. It was a very low-lying valley, probably the old course of the Jordan before it was checked at the Dead Sea, and so shut in by red sandstone mountains as to be stiflingly oppressive when

the southern sun poured upon the breathless
atmosphere and the soil of the broken sand
débris from the mountains. There was
water, for the stream that had come forth at
Meribah ran on to find an issue into the
Gulf of Akabah, but murmurings at the
course indicated by the Pillar, and even at
Moses, began to be heard. Angry sighs
were everywhere.

'Oh, silence, silence! Somathah,' cried
Egla, 'or we shall bring down a judgment
on us again.'

A scream interrupted her. The mur-
murer was shaking his foot, to which adhered
a snake about two feet long, with little horns
on its nose, and spots of reddish-yellow along
its sides. It had lain coiled in the sand, in
a print of a camel's foot, and had actually
reared up and leapt at the foot of the
unhappy man, who fell and expired in less
than half an hour. From that time the fatal
bites were frequent; the serpents lay half
hidden in the sand, and bit as soon as

disturbed, or what was worse coiled themselves up and came darting at their un-
fortunate victims. The animals were full of
dread of them and could hardly be made to
pass their lairs, and though the onward journey was continued day by day, so as to get
beyond this perilous region, the losses were
very considerable, and it was in fear and
dread that the manna-gatherers went out in
the morning, sure to see some of their
number either writhing in convulsions or
in the numb torpor that more gently put an
end to their lives. Enhat's wife had thus
died, and a child of Zemira's, and the people
in general suffered far more; but, unlike
former times, they assembled before the
Tabernacle, not to cry out against Moses,
but to beg him to entreat the Lord to save
them from these deadly creatures.

A day or two later, from the tents that
had been set up on a slight rising ground in
the hope of avoiding the snakes, Axa perceived something above the gate of the

court, and looking more intently, she saw
that it was a tall pole, with something upon
it which glistened in the sunset. Almost at
the same time Ulim and his sons came back
from the Tabernacle, making proclamation,
'In mercy and forgiveness for the sin of
Israel, the Lord hath vouchsafed to cause
that Moses should make yonder a serpent of
brass, and set it on a pole, that so, if a
serpent have bitten any man, if he behold
the serpent of brass, he liveth.'

'What power to heal can there be in
gazing on a brazen figure?' exclaimed Enhat.

'I have seen,' responded Mirglip. 'As we
returned from the council of the elders, we
saw a Benjamite lying helpless and nigh
unto death. We bade him take hope and
look up. My father held up his head, and
presently the blackness left his lips, he was
able to walk, and we left him on his way to
his tent.'

'And my poor blameless wife died without the hope of your remedy,' sighed Enhat;

'such blind belief is beyond me. Rather I should suppose that the venom of the snake was exhausted.'

But that night, as Enhat lay down in his tent, a cry told that he had felt the poisoned tooth. He started forth, grasping the reptile by the neck to take it from among his children, but fell as he passed the door. Adoram, Mirglip, and Dumah were with him at once. He was the companion of their infancy, and they loved him.

'Look up! look up!' cried Mirglip, setting his bare foot on the horned head of the serpent, only regardless of the sting so far as to keep his eye steadfastly on the pole with the brazen serpent, which stood out, darkly visible in front of the flaming pillar, but with the edges lighted from behind. 'Look up, Enhat. Open thine eyes. Call on the Lord for mercy! Look and live.'

'Look and live!' echoed the brothers.

'Folly! magic! The sting was slight. I'll not,' began Enhat, closing his eyes; and then he wavered and fell into Dumah's arms. The torpor was already coming on, nor could any effort rouse him, and thus he lay till his eyes were closed for ever, and the family mourned over him, as much for his obduracy and want of faith as for the untimely death that cut him off from the Land of Promise.

Mirglip stumbled into his tent to be tended by Axa, in thankfulness, for there were no symptoms of death creeping on him, though the wound in his heel was very painful, and so continued for several days.

But the next morning, while leading the little children to gather the manna, Sherah saw a serpent springing at little Huldah, and while trying to shield her, was bitten. That moment Dumah and Zuriel both hurried to her, sustained her wavering step and bore her beyond the tents where she could see the serpent on the pole; while Egla carried the sobbing crying child, bidding her look up and pointing the way.

The child seemed to recover at once when

she had once been persuaded to open her
eyes and look, saying after the mother,
'God have mercy.'   Soon she turned round
with a smile, stretched out her little finger,
pointed at the serpent now gilded by the
rising sun, murmured her broken word for
pretty, laid her head on her mother's shoulder
and fell asleep, the colour coming back to her
cheeks.

But Sherah lay in a sort of trance with
her head on Zuriel's lap.   They were sure
that she had looked, for she had whispered
a word or two of prayer, and clasped her
hands as they laid her down, and indeed her
eyes were not entirely closed, but the stillness was such that it might be the perilous
slumber, and Ulim and Axa had time to
come from the tents and kneel beside her in
fervent prayer before there was any sign of
revival.   Ulim bade them not fear, the promise could not fail, and he showed them
that there was a wonderful look of gladness
spreading over her features.   Was it the

smile of death? Nay, the lips parted with
joy, the eyes opened and shone on Ulim,
and as he put a piece of manna in her mouth
the recovery set in. She sat up, clasped her
hands again, and said, 'Thanks and praise,
O God my Redeemer!' and then rose,
declaring herself healed, and that she must
give praise within the court of the Tabernacle.

'Was it a serpent of brass that I saw
hanging on yonder cross?' she said, 'or was
it the dazzling of mine eyes? for what I beheld changed from the thing of evil to a
Face, full of pain and sorrow indeed, but of
infinite patience, sweetness, goodness, and all
the pain of my heart seemed to leave me, as
though He drew it to Himself and took
the serpent's sting. Oh when shall I see
Him again?'

CHAPTER IV

IN SIGHT

The great and terrible land
Of wilderness and drought
Lay in the shadows behind us,
For the Lord had brought us out:
Till we pitched our tent at last,
   The desert done,
When we saw the hills of the Holy Land
Gleam to our sinking sun.

Ezekiel, by B. M.

WITH the serpents of the Arabah, the worst was over; the Israelites had come beyond the mountains of Edom into the gentler valleys clothed with verdure to the north thereof, namely to the fertile pasture land where the innumerable flocks of the Moabites were driven down to feed in the summer.

Such greenness of grass, such shade of trees, was exquisite to the weary travellers.

To the elders it recalled the richness of
Egypt after a flood, to the younger it
was all wonder and delight, and songs of
joy were echoing from one encampment
to another at each new discovery of delight.

Their first well, especially, not the spring
of the wilderness, but a real well dug by
themselves, was rejoiced over and sung over,
as an earnest of the settled life preparing for
them.

The beauty of the whole region was great,
though they were only skirting the Moabite
country, and had been denied a passage
through the land which they were not to
invade, as they claimed kindred through Lot.
Moreover, it was needful to ascend the river
Arnon till it narrowed enough for the crossing of the people, for there was a very rapid
stream as it rushed down the great gorge,
or cañon as it now would be called, leading
to the Dead Sea, of whose intense blue they
obtained glimpses as they passed the heights.

Here, however, came news that Sihon, king of Heshbon, not only refused passage through his territories, but that he had united with Og, the huge king of Bashan, to oppose the further progress of the tribes.

The fighting men were called out to make an expedition against these kings before they should attack the camp. Joshua, now prince of Ephraim, instead of his grandfather Elishama, was their leader, and with him went all the younger men of the Ben Beriah, except Mirglip who was still lame from the wound in his foot.

He was the less grieved at missing the campaign because his father, the good old Ulim, was manifestly failing. He much missed his old friend Elishama, and had never been quite the same man since the sentence had gone forth against Moses, whom he loved and revered with all his heart ; and, though he never complained, the struggle up the Arabah ground had tried him severely, and when the smoother, more genial land was

reached, what brought refreshment to others
only brought languor to him.   After bidding
farewell to Adoram, Zemira, Dumah, and
the grandsons now of an age for war, his
strength rapidly failed, nor could Sherah and
the rest wonder, for he was one of the last
men who had been above forty years old
when the fatal defection had taken place;
but he had never expected to be spared,
though, trusting to his blameless life, they
had begun to hope for him, till they saw him
manifestly sinking.   The rule which made
man's life at fourscore years 'a labour and
a sorrow,' had not yet set in, and there were
some in the camp, Levites and women, besides Joshua and Caleb, who exceeded that
age, and were still in their full strength and
vigour, but Ulim was more than ninety years
old, and the burden of his years oppressed
him.   The repose of the camp during the
expedition to the north was very welcome,
but it did not restore him, and he lay where
he could see the guiding pillar above the

sanctuary, murmuring to himself words of
prayer and praise, and often Jacob's beautiful blessing to Joseph :

The Almighty, who shall bless thee
With blessings of Heaven above,
The blessings of thy Father
Have prevailed above the blessings of thy progenitors
Unto the utmost bound of the everlasting hills.

His eyes wandered to the blue, indistinct
distance, where hills on the horizon were
blended with clouds, and he repeated again
and again :

'The utmost bound of the everlasting hills.'

Joshua was away with the army, and
Mirglip had to act as an elder.   He told
Moses of his father's state, and the mighty
and holy lawgiver came down to the tent
to see and bless his faithful follower.   ·

In his white garments, with his long snowy
beard and hoary head, somewhat of the
radiance of Mount Horeb still lingering
about his eyes, Sherah looked up to him in

wonder and awe, all the more that there was a sadness about his face, as he stood by the mat on which Ulim lay looking up to him with a rapt gaze, though perhaps not fully conscious of things of earth, for instead of greeting, or attempting to join in the women's acts of obeisance, he continued his murmur of

'The utmost bound of the everlasting hills,'

and Moses took up the words and added to them :

'Blessings unto the utmost bound of the everlasting hills,
And for the good will of Him that dwelt in the bush.'

Laying his hand upon the head of Ulim, he blessed the old man solemnly, and the mourners with him, then left them. Axa and Egla gazed long after his receding figure, brightened by the evening sun, and when they turned back to the tent, Sherah was closing the eyes of the brother-in-law who had been so long her guide and stay.

Mirglip buried him in one of the caves of Abarim, the mountains between the camp and Moab, and the Ben Beriah mourned for their elder, as men and women might mourn not without hope, but with that hope still undefined and imperfect.

CHAPTER V

CONQUEST BEGINNING

Must not those hands, which heavenward raised, made wreck
Of the proud hopes of stubborn Amalek,
Which bowed pale Bashan's thousands in the fight,
And crushed the aspiring crest of Sihon's might,—
Must not those hands, with vengeance not their own,
Tear haughty Canaan from his guilty throne?

M. ROLLESTON.

THE encampment tarried long in the hills and land around the Arnon, covering several miles, while victories were won by their warriors. The first was over Sihon, the Amorite king of Heshbon, who was killed in the battle, and it was followed up by the conquest of all his cities, in a very beautiful and fertile district. Many of the troops took their families with them and encamped in the meadows of the newly-won ground. Then followed an attack by the

gigantic Og, king of Bashan, who fell in
fight, after which all his seventy cities were
reduced, strong as they were.   His bedstead,
which probably means his sarcophagus, was
preserved as a token of his huge stature.
Adoram was one of the comparatively few
Israelites who were killed in this war, and
Zemira could not but be thankful that his
father was no longer on earth to be grieved
by his loss.   The troops came back delighted
with the country they had subdued.   It was
most beautiful, with meadow-land watered
by brooks, and full of splendid cattle, with
woods of fine oak and cork trees on the
rising grounds.   Bashan, moreover, had a
curious natural sort of fortification of its own
to the northward in tremendous cliffs of
granite and basaltic rock, which ascended
like a wall from the rich green lands
below, where seventy cities had been built of
blocks of stone therefrom, the very doors
and shutters of the windows cut out and
moving on grooves, and yet the panic of the

natives had rendered them an easy prey
when once they had lost their king.

And here it was that the Reubenites,
Gadites, and the descendants of Gilead, a
son of Manasseh, wished to take up their
final abode. Moses was at first averse to
the plan, both as separating them from the
other tribes, and making them more liable
to invasion, and as diminishing the force
which was to invade the land of Canaan ;
but they undertook to send their fighting
men to assist the rest of the host, leaving
their families and cattle in the strong-
holds which they had already begun to
occupy, and a guard free from encumbrances
would be a distinct advantage to the army.
The other objection was, by divine direction,
to be overruled, though the result in later
times proved that these were the tribes most
endangered and the first to fall.

The long residence in this pleasant land
beyond Moab led to more intercourse with
the desert tribes of the vicinity than was

altogether good for the people, and Mirglip, who had become the authority among the Ben Beriah, did not obtain so much submission as his father had done. The nephews, sons of Adoram and Zemira, were hardy warriors, grown rude and reckless in their plundering campaigns, and what vexed him most was the conduct and defection of Dumah.

In his first marriage, though it had begun in eager affection, Dumah had been disappointed. Keren's heart had been with her brother and his aims, and afterwards with his children, and she had scarcely been a wife to him. Helah, whom he had afterwards married, was a proud, contentious woman, determined to assert that her own tribe of Judah was the prime family destined to the birthright and despising the other tribes. She was jealous of Keren, and afterwards of all the duty and affection that Dumah and his children paid to his good old mother. Sherah ended by taking up her abode with her daughter Axa, much to her son's mortification, but the wrangling tongues in his own tent were not silenced, and he was little there.   Even his mother had small power over him in these days.   Helah had destroyed her influence for good, without obtaining much real power of her own, except over her children, and latterly over two slaves whom, contrary to orders, Dumah had brought back with him from Heshbon.

Axa was much angered, and would have spent half the day in angry words towards her brother and Helah, but her mother silenced both her and Egla.   'It is the lot of the aged to be set aside, daughters,' she said; 'nor will Dumah be brought back if women's tongues make a storm around him! We will not drive him away by reproaches, but rather pray that he may see the danger of his ways.'

'It is the Midianites that he has made friends with,' said Egla.

'And are not Hobab and his clan the friends of Moses?' said Sherah.

'Nay,' said Egla, 'but they have been visited by their kindred, idolaters, who are allied with the Moabites.'

'Yea,' said Axa. 'Heard you not Zuriel tell that they are wondrous horsemen, with the most wise and fleet and beautiful steeds that ever were seen ?'

'Moses bade our nation not to trust in horses nor to use them in war.'

'I trow,' said Axa, 'that is what serves to tempt Dumah. He loved a horse even in Egypt.'

'Ay,' said Egla, 'and I have heard him murmur at the command, that Moses was too old to judge what was best for younger men in a new country.'

'Alas! alas!' said Axa; 'alas for my brother that he should turn aside on the very borders of the land, he, who might go into it to possess it. Thou mindest, mother, he was but eighteen years old at the numbering at Mount Sinai.'

'Ah! may our prayers win him back,'

sighed Sherah. Better so than to talk of
his errors. My son, the one son I saved
from Pharaoh's cruelty, the son redeemed
by the blood of the Passover! It cannot be
that he should be led astray as a man
waxing old, when his youth was pure and
true.'

Axa could not help throwing a gesture of
enmity towards Helah's tent, as the cause
of all the wrong; but before Egla had
spoken out the same thought, Mirglip,
Zuriel, and Dumah advanced together, and
it was plain that they brought tidings, as all,
with the reverence of their breeding, bent in
greeting to the mother in Israel.

'We have heard tidings, mother,' began
Mirglip; 'evil tidings.'

'Oh, not so, my father,' cried Zuriel,
'since what do they mean but that we shall
deal with Moab as we have dealt with
Heshbon and Bashan?'

'We were forbidden to meddle with Moab,
our kinsman,' said Sherah, 'and king Balak

hath not molested our camps, though he denied passage to our host.'

'Ah! but wherefore?' said Dumah. 'Because he hath been biding his time. In alarm at our conquests of Sihon and Og, he thinks Moses a powerful enchanter, and while we were absent in the north, hath been sending even to the great river Euphrates, on swift dromedaries, to fetch a diviner who may, he thinks, overcome the power of Moses by his skill in winning away the favour of the Lord from him and from us.'

'In ignorance,' said Zuriel. 'Mother, wife, fear him not.'

'Yet,' said Dumah, 'true it is that this Balaam the son of Beor is a worshipper of our own God, the Lord Jehovah, and knows that we are His chosen. Twice, as they say, he refused to come, and when at last he consented on the promise of great rewards, strange marvels as it seems stood in his way, but he overcame them, and is now at Peor with Balak, prepared to do all to defy Moses and his God.'

'Let him try!' said Mirglip scornfully.

''Tis true the magicians of Egypt could not stand before him,' said Dumah, 'but this man comes not in the name of Chemosh. He worships our God.'

'O Dumah, my son, hast thou so little faith in the God of all the earth as to think He can be turned aside from His people by a few incantations of a magician?' exclaimed Sherah. 'Where is thy faith?'

'Where is his faith? That's what I say,' burst in Helah's shrill voice. 'He is losing every shred of it by hankering after all the lewd idle fellows in the camp, Simeonites and Danites, and all the rest—not to speak of Midianites and their wiles. Come home, thou recreant, and drive back the old he-goat that is as wicked a truant as thyself, or we shall have contention with the vaga-bond fellows of Benjamin. That is what comes of bringing home Amorite slaves.'

And she drove Dumah away, while the others looked at each other in dismay, thinking that it was no wonder that he resorted to other company.

Once indeed they had a distant view of this much-dreaded enchanter, on a peak above their portion of the camp. They saw a crowd of Moabites above, and a heaping together of large stones, so as to construct seven rude altars at regular distances, and they could see the flame and smoke of the sacrifices that took place on them, and now and then, on the wind, came the yelling refrain of Moabitish hymns, and the beating of some sort of drum in imprecation. Some of the women cowered in dread, but Sherah and Axa cried shame on them for their small trust in their own God.

Then they saw, as the smoke was blown aside, a wild figure with hair and beard floating on the wind, stretching out his arms towards the tents. They could see presently, when the smoke grew less, the sun glancing

on a crowned form beside him, which Zemira
who had been on an embassy to him, told
them was no other than king Balak, and
there was no mistaking his furious gestures
of wrath and disappointment.

By and by, through the Midianite relatives
of Hobab, came the full knowledge that
every incantation had been vain, and instead
of the expected curses, nothing but the very
choicest blessings had been poured forth
from Balaam's tongue, to the utter discomfiture and rage of Balak. Fragments of
his words were even repeated among the
Israelites. Above all, ' There shall come a
Star out of Jacob, and a Sceptre shall rise out
of Israel, and shall smite all the corners of
Moab '

CHAPTER VI

THE LAST DEFECTION

The land before you
Is open, win your way and take your rest,
So sounds your war-note, but your path of glory
By many a cloud is darkened and unblest.

KEBLE.

HELAH had learnt that the soothsayer, while gazing on the lion standard of Judah, had said, 'Behold the people shall rise as a lion,' echoing the prophecy of Jacob, 'Judah is a lion's whelp,' in honour of which she had named her son Aryah. There are those who will turn even inspiration to their hurt, and her pride was increased by the augury as she accepted it, so that her tent became more unhomelike to Dumah than ever.

It would have been well if he had sought that of his mother and sister for comfort, instead of wandering wherever he could find amusement.   Nor did he show himself willing to join Mirglip and the other elders of his tribe, who were delivering to those who gladly listened the counsels of Moses, summing up and repeating much of what had been formerly delivered to him at Mount Sinai, and adding details thereto, with prophetic insight into the future temptations and difficulties in the settled life which he would never enjoy.

Dumah declared that he had heard all this law before, and had no mind for the repetition thereof.   He, with others of the somewhat demoralised wanderers, spent a good deal of time in watching where, on the Abarim mountains, the tents of the Midianites were gathering, especially towards the hill of Peor as a centre.

It was understood that there was a shrine on this mountain to Baal Peor, the lord of nature and of fertility, and that a periodical festival of the Midianitish tribes was to be held there conjointly with the Moabites.   A sheikh, riding one of the splendid Arabian horses, had actually come down to invite the family of Hobab to join in the national festival, and the Israelites to be spectators.

'But,' said Zuriel, who brought home the information, 'the sons of Hobab indignantly refused, as worshippers of the one Lord Jehovah.'

'Nay,' argued Rogel, the son of Adoram and Malbeth, 'they told us that it was the same God whom they worshipped — Him who made heaven and earth, only they call Him by His name of Baal, the lord. They too are the children of Abraham, and though we have one ritual, why should we not behold theirs, all offered to the same?'

'And what a ritual!' said Zuriel, 'a ritual of drunkenness and revelry. Never, never would the pure One Lord Jehovah permit, far less enjoin, such so-called worship.'

'So thou hearest,' said Rogel.

'Ay, from old Hobab, whose father Jethro abhorred the foul rites.'

'What sayest thou, Dumah?' said Rogel, seeing the elder man approaching, 'is not Zuriel over harsh and strict?'

'He saith even as Moses interpreted,' said Dumah, 'and I hear the fresh edicts are stricter still; but I see not that if Baal be indeed only another name for Adonai, the Lord, why we should not look on at a kindred worship, when we can avoid all share in the excess, or whatever is unholy.'

Dumah was still speaking when a sound of singing was heard, with the musical clash of cymbals between, and there danced upon the open space before the tents, hand in hand in unison, with foot and foot moving in rhythm, a troop of girls in the brilliancy of Arab beauty.

> Their limbs were fashioned fair and free
> In nature's justest symmetry,
> And wreath'd with flowers, with odours graced,
> Their raven ringlets reached their waist.
> In Eastern pomp, the henna pale
> Its gilding lent each shapely nail,
> And the dark sumah gave the eye
> More liquid and more lustrous dye.

Their hair and their waists were wreathed
with vine - leaves, and their song was an
alluring persuasion, which seemed to madden
the young men, who sprang up and danced
with the same impulse of the music.   Even
the children with their little bare feet began
to join the dance as by witchcraft impelled.
Only Zuriel caught up his children, one in
each arm, and dashed back with them
crying and screaming to Egla in the tent.
Helah was rushing out to seize upon Aryah,
and to call with loud threats upon her husband.

At the same moment, returning from the
Tabernacle, Mirglip was seen, and with him
Asaph and some of the Levite guard.   Stern
and angry he stood, lifting his staff, and
threatening, breaking into the inviting chant
with the rebuke :

'Away with you, daughters of evil, away
with you and your unholy songs, ere the
Levite guard chase you.   The camp of the
Lord is not to be defiled with idols.   Away,
sorceresses !'

The girls tried to laugh and drown his words with their song, but he said, loud enough for all to hear, 'It is by command of Moses! Sons of Ephraim, sons of Levi, draw your bows.'

The girls began to move away, still dancing, for they were brave girls, but with them, woven into their dance, went Rogel and several more of the youths. Mirglip called after them to return, sharply saying, 'Inhospitality cannot be brooked.' Dumah was following, not in the dance, but still drawn along by the attraction, and deaf to Mirglip's entreaty, 'Dumah, my brother, forbear, come back, listen.'

His voice was lost in Helah's shriek of abuse, as, putting down Aryah, she flew after her husband, overwhelming him with vituperations, and wildly recalling him. She grasped his garment, grappled with him, struck him. It was the less wonder that he returned the blow, shook himself free, and her shrieks, half of anger, half of despair, echoed on the retreating cadences of the Midianite song.

Mirglip raised her, and tried to bid her turn to pray that Dumah's better mind might return at sight of what the rites of Baal Peor really were, but she would do nothing but tear her hair and rend her clothes, and broke away from him, calling herself the most miserable being in the camp.

Sorrowfully did the rest turn back to their tents, and Mirglip said, 'This is the device of the soothsayer. God would not forsake Israel while He saw no iniquity in them, and now he hath counselled the sending these women to tempt our young men away from their faith to the Lord Jehovah, that so He may be offended and abandon them to the rage of the Moabites.'

'Woe is me, my son,' sighed Sherah. 'Child of so many hopes and fears and cares, to be led astray at last!'

'Oh for my father's hand of power!' chimed in Mirglip.

'That the young men should be led aside by the charms of those maidens is not wonderful,' said Axa, 'but for Dumah, grown almost old——'

'I fear me,' said Mirglip, 'when the aids of our youth are gone, that even in age there come fresh temptations and trials to those that expect them not. And poor Dumah hath never had a happy home. My heart is sad for him. He was the brother of my heart.'

'We can but pray for him,' said Sherah; 'we will go to the Tabernacle and offer a kid of the flock for his transgression.'

Those ensuing days were a time of grief and anxiety in the camp. Dumah and Rogel and the rest did not return, and Helah, in her wrath, would not join in the offering, declaring that her faithless husband did not deserve it from her, and she removed herself and her boy to her father's tent in the tribe of Judah, which was encamped to the north, farthest away from the Peor

x

mountain, with the Tabernacle between.
Ephraim, to the eastward, could hear upon
the morning breeze the clash of the drums
and cymbals and the echo of the songs,
sometimes fierce and warlike, but more often
in mad revelry.

It was the southern division, Reuben,
Simeon, and Gad, whose camp lay nearest
to the mount of temptation, and there was
only too much reason to think that many
of the Simeonites had been led away and
absolutely maddened by the orgies of the
Midianites, which continued day after day,
and grew louder, wilder, and more drunken
every night.

Suddenly, however, cries began to be
heard, the sounds of revelry were broken
by howls. A deadly sudden disease had
broken out, brought perhaps (as men would
say) by the foul habits of some of the
wandering tribes, and aggravated by the
horrid excesses in which all were indulging,
but thus most truly the judicial scourge of

the avenging God.   Moses had already sent
forth the decree that the apostates, who had
joined themselves to Baal Peor and were
wallowing in his horrible orgies, should be
put to death by the judges of Israel, ere
they could corrupt the rest.   And Mirglip
turned pale as he heard it with the thought
of the beloved ones whom he might be called
on to execute.   But even as he came nigh to
the tents of the Ben Beriah, a form reeled
forward before him — one that he knew,
though the mantle was torn and wine-
stained, and a withered crown of vine leaves
hung on one side of the head.   Staggering
on, the wretched figure dropped at Sherah's
feet, and stretching out an exhausted hand
sighed out, 'Pardon, mother—God, pardon—'
rolled over in a convulsion and died.

Bitter, bitter was the sorrow of Sherah
over her only son, and of Axa over her
brother, fallen in his sin when the Land of
Rest was almost won.

The chief comfort that came to her was

a message sent to her by Moses—'God *may* pardon even while He punishes the sin.'

The sin was punished indeed, at once by the deadly sickness which cut off the offenders, above all in the camp of Simeon, and by the swords of the judges of Israel, especially of the young priest Phinehas. The plague did not cease till fully a third of the Simeonites, especially the guilty ones, had perished, and he had not only signalised his zeal by slaying one of their worst offenders, who was likewise highest in rank, but as a priest had offered his passionate intercession that the people might once more be spared and forgiven.

Mirglip and Zuriel had not to dip their swords in kindred blood. Rogel and the rest never returned. They must have been struck down in the midst of their excesses on the mountain.

Zuriel, however, was one of the thousand contributed by Ephraim, as well as the other tribes, to go forth for the punishment of

Midian, when their chief leaders were cut off, and Balaam fell among them, the victim of his own covetousness, against his better knowledge, so that the most piteous irony is connected with his inspired wish—'Let me die the death of the righteous, and let my last end be like his.'

CHAPTER VII

MOSES' FAREWELL

Know ye not our glorious Leader
Salem may but see and die ;
Israel's guide, and nurse, and feeder,
Israel's hope from far must eye :
Then departing,
Find a worthier home on high.

KEBLE.

PARTING and sorrow are the heritage of old
age. Some have fallen beside us in youth
when the spirits are strong, and the wound
ceases to be a sore, but rather a scar, nay,
almost a jewel-mark. Some are taken away
in middle age, having made half their journey,
and dropping with more or less hope of the
mark ; and some go from us, for whom we
have striven and grieved and longed to guide
along with us ; and, lastly, some, the dear

companions and the venerated lamps who
have led and brightened our whole lifetime,
go from us, and leave us lonely.

So it was known that 'the master was to
be taken from the head' of Israel. Joshua
knew it full well. Mirglip had seen him
come forth from before the door of the holy
place, his noble head bowed down, and his
eyes full of tears, as he felt the weight of the
charge handed on to him so solemnly. He
was to win the land, and his watchword was
ever to be, 'Be strong and of a good
courage'; so should he enter into that land
which Moses had toiled for. 'Shew thy
servants thy work, and their children thy
glory' was to be fulfilled.

The Book of the Law, including the
revealed narrative of the Creation, the Flood,
and the history of the Patriarchs, had been
written out by Zerah, Asaph, and other
Levites on rolls of skins of parchment, as
well as on tablets of stretched papyrus; the
last for common use, but the parchments

were solemnly committed to the priests, to
be laid up in the ark of the covenant.   There
was a charge to read and explain them to
the people at every Feast of the Tabernacles,
that thus their obligations might never be
forgotten.

Then for the last time the elders of the
tribes were convened around the Tabernacle,
and beyond them were gathered the people,
pressing into the open space, intent upon
those last words, which the voice and tongue,
once weak and slow, but now strong and
unbroken by age, chanted forth in stanzas
repeated and sung forth in like manner by
the elders, the song expressive of God's
bounty and greatness and confessing Israel's
perverseness, and the prophetic blessing,
taking up that of the dying Jacob and
carrying it on to the tribes.

The echoes of the song had not died away
when the majestic man in white robes, his face
shining as with renewed light, began to move
forward attended by Eleazar and Joshua.

The elders all bowed down, veiling their heads and weeping sorely as he held out his hands over them and blessed them, with special words to those who had come nearest to him, Mirglip among them.

Then he moved on in like manner through the congregation, all bending down or lying prostrate.   As he passed the tents of the Ben Beriah, Sherah's aged tearful face and clasped hands were raised, and he paused to lay his hand on her brow and say, 'The Lord comfort thee, my sister, and give thee rest.'   And as Axa dared to hold up to him Zuriel's youngest babe, he likewise touched the little thing's brow and blessed it.

When, with weeping eyes, the women could look up again, the white figure, with the same majestic port, and step showing no trace of his hundred and twenty years, had gone on, but he had left a strange new calm and sense of hope with the bereaved Sherah.

Joshua and Eleazar walked with him, the

seventy elders followed at a distance, Mir-glip among them. By and by, on the green slopes of Mount Nebo, the mass of moving, ascending forms could be discerned — one figure, gleaming white, going on up the steeps above—and the faithful priest and captain keeping near. But more and more did they fade in the distance. At last, on one lofty peak, in the clear air, the sunset beams lighted up once more the snow-white figure seen against the red-purple hill.

A cloud, catching the gold of the sun-beams, descended. The straining eyes saw no more.

By and by, long after the night had closed in and the stars were shining overhead, Mir-glip came back. He could tell little more. He with the other elders had tarried where the grass gave place to the rocks. Moses had blessed them and bidden them come no farther. They knelt or lay prostrate there they knew not how long, till Joshua and Eleazar returned. They too had watched,

from another point, as Moses gazed over the
land he was permitted to see but not possess.
Then they saw him turn as to descend into
a ravine, but therewith the white cloud closed
over him, and they saw him no more.

> O lonely grave in Moab's land,
>   O dark Bethpeor's hill,
> Speak to these curious hearts of ours,
>   And teach them to be still !
> God hath His mysteries of grace,
>   Ways that we cannot tell ;
> He hides them deep, like the hidden sleep
>   Of him He loved so well.

'Never, never will there be such another,'
was Axa's sigh.

'Nay, not of mere earth, may be,' said
her husband. 'Yet were not his words,
"The Lord thy God will raise up unto thee
a Prophet from the midst of thee, of thy
brethren, like unto me ; unto Him shall ye
hearken "' ?

'Oh, how, how hearken to any save
Moses ?' sighed Axa.

'Nay, my daughter,' said Sherah. 'Something tells me that though we may tarry long, long, that prophet may be the Star of Jacob, the Sceptre of Judah, the Shepherd of Israel, the Seed of the woman.'

CHAPTER VIII

REST

I have come to call thee home,
  Said our veiled guest ;
The terrible journey of life is done,
  I will take thee to thy rest.

B. M.

IT was a lovely evening in spring, and an
awning sheltered the top of the two-storied
house, securely built of stone, in which
Sherah lay, on palm-leaf mats, further shaded
by the trellis work on which the young leaves
of a vine were spread in their rich beauty,
while the broad foliage of a fig-tree just
reached to the flat roof, surrounded by a low
railing on which roses and creepers were
trained. There was a court below into which
the cows and goats would be driven when

needed; and there was a massive wall of stone around the whole village, with a deep arched gateway, under which Mirglip sat to do justice.

Beyond lay cornfields, amber - coloured, partly falling before the reaper, partly built up into sheaves, and some with the evening wind blowing over them. Grey-leaved olives grew among them ; the sloping pastures were brightened with crimson anemones, which, when the breeze stirred the long grass, shone out fitfully like a river of radiance as they lay on the slopes ; while sheep and white oxen grazed on the open patches, and streams and brooks shone out here and there between the meadows. A soft, gentle, misty atmosphere gave an exquisite colouring ; and as the sun went lower the northern ridge of hills was tinted with deep purple—the ridge in which could be distinguished at no great distance, over the woods of oak and terebinth which shut in the vale, the gap formed by the terraced hills of Ebal and Gerizim. Ebal with the sharp, bare cliffs, one of which was

inscribed with the Ten Commandments, the
other, in more gentle outlines,—the mounts
of cursing and of blessing.   And above and
beyond all, rising into the sky, were the
snowy points of Hermon, the cold of which
sent down the freshening dews and rains.

For this was Timnath Serah, in the midst
of the portion that Jacob gave to his son
Joseph ; and the Ben Beriah possessed a
part of it by right of inheritance, and would
hold it in peace and gladness for two cen-
turies before the evil days of apostasy and
bloodshed.   The wondrous beauty of the
place was the fulfilment of the promises of
God to His people.

So did Sherah and her children feel it.
All since that parting with Moses had gone
by her like a dream : the journey and return
of the spies, and the wonderful crossing of
the river Jordan, when the rapid stream
stood still, and the stony bed lay dry, with
the Ark of the Covenant upborne by the
priests standing still in the midst.

As she was carried in an ox waggon over the rugged bed, she looked across at the foaming waters piled up to the north, and said to Axa, against whom she was leaning, 'Even so was the Red Sea. To us, this is the passage to our rest; to the young ones, the washing to dedicate them to the captain of the wars of the Lord.'

Of the camp at Gilgal and the warlike expeditions and conquests she knew little, though her grandson Zuriel distinguished himself greatly in the command of his 'thousand' of Ephraimites. She only knew that the Lord's promises of victory were realised, and she gave thanks.

For her sake Mirglip and Axa rejoiced that Joshua settled them at once in his own fenced village of Timnath Serah, the place of the sun, nor did the family share in the discontent of others of the tribe, who feared to attack the giants of the further forest-clad mountains.

Mirglip, Zuriel, and Egla were gone up

to Shiloh with Joshua, to offer the first sheaf at the Passover feast; taking with them for the first time Zuriel's eldest boy, and driving with them the white unblemished lamb that was to serve for the feast. Axa remained to watch over her mother, whose breath came short and laboured, so that they had laid her on the flat roof to breathe the evening air.

Silently she lay, with clasped hands. Only as the first pale star shone in the west, she raised herself a little and exclaimed, 'They are slaying the Lamb of Redemption! Glory be to God who has led us out, and brought us to our Rest—Rest—oh, Rest!'

She lay back, and Axa knew that she had entered into her rest.

THE END

UNIFORM EDITION OF THE NOVELS AND TALES OF

CHARLOTTE M. YONGE.

In Crown 8vo, Cloth extra.   Illustrated.   3s. 6d. each.

1. THE HEIR OF REDCLYFFE.
2. HEARTSEASE.
3. HOPES AND FEARS.
4. DYNEVOR TERRACE.
5. THE DAISY CHAIN.
6. THE TRIAL: More Links of the Daisy Chain.
7. PILLARS OF THE HOUSE.   Vol. I.
8. PILLARS OF THE HOUSE.   Vol. II.
9. THE YOUNG STEPMOTHER.
10. THE CLEVER WOMAN OF THE FAMILY.
11. THE THREE BRIDES.
12. MY YOUNG ALCIDES.
13. THE CAGED LION.
14. THE DOVE IN THE EAGLE'S NEST.
15. THE CHAPLET OF PEARLS.
16. LADY HESTER AND THE DANVERS PAPERS.
17. MAGNUM BONUM.
18. LOVE AND LIFE.
19. UNKNOWN TO HISTORY.
20. STRAY PEARLS.
21. THE ARMOURER'S 'PRENTICES.
22. THE TWO SIDES OF THE SHIELD.
23. NUTTIE'S FATHER.
24. SCENES AND CHARACTERS.
25. CHANTRY HOUSE.
26. A MODERN TELEMACHUS.
27. BYE-WORDS.
28. BEECHCROFT AT ROCKSTONE.
29. A REPUTED CHANGELING.
30. MORE BYE-WORDS.
31. THE LITTLE DUKE.
32. THE PRINCE AND THE PAGE.
33. THE LANCES OF LYNWOOD.
34. P's AND Q's, AND LITTLE LUCY'S WONDERFUL GLOBE.
35. THE TWO PENNILESS PRINCESSES.
36. THAT STICK.
37. AN OLD WOMAN'S OUTLOOK IN A HAMPSHIRE VILLAGE.
38. GRISLY GRISELL; or, The Laidly Lady of Whitburn.   A Tale of the Wars of the Roses.

MACMILLAN AND CO., LTD., LONDON.

MACMILLAN'S THREE-AND-SIXPENNY LIBRARY.

Crown 8vo.   3s. 6d. each volume.

By CHARLES DICKENS.

The Pickwick Papers.
Oliver Twist.
Nicholas Nickleby.
Martin Chuzzlewit.
The Old Curiosity Shop.
Barnaby Rudge.
Dombey and Son.

Christmas Books.
Sketches by Boz.
David Copperfield.
American Notes and Pictures from Italy.
The Letters of Charles Dickens.
Bleak House.

By BRET HARTE.

SPEAKER.—"The best work of Mr. Bret Harte stands entirely alone . . . . marked on every page by distinction and quality. . . . Strength and delicacy, spirit and tenderness, go together in his best work."

Cressy.

The Heritage of Dedlow Marsh.

A First Family of Tasajara.

By THOMAS HUGHES.

Tom Brown's Schooldays. With Illustrations by A. HUGHES and S. P. HALL.
Tom Brown at Oxford. With Illustrations by S. P. HALL.

The Scouring of the White Horse, and The Ashen Faggot. With Illustrations by RICHARD DOYLE.

By HENRY JAMES.

SATURDAY REVIEW.—"He has the power of seeing with the artistic perception of the few, and of writing about what he has seen, so that the many can understand and feel with him."
WORLD.—"His touch is so light, and his humour, while shrewd and keen, so free from bitterness."

A London Life. | The Aspern Papers, etc. | The Tragic Muse.

By ANNIE KEARY.

SPECTATOR.—"In our opinion there have not been many novels published better worth reading. The literary workmanship is excellent, and all the windings of the stories are worked with patient fulness and a skill not often found."

Castle Daly.
A York and a Lancaster Rose.
Oldbury.

A Doubting Heart.
Janet's Home.
Nations around Israel.

By W. CLARK RUSSELL.

TIMES.—"Mr. Clark Russell is one of those writers who have set themselves to revive the British sea story in all its glorious excitement. Mr. Russell has made a considerable reputation in this line. His plots are well conceived, and that of 'Marooned' is no exception to this rule."

Marooned. | A Strange Elopement.

MACMILLAN AND CO., LTD., LONDON.

MACMILLAN'S THREE-AND-SIXPENNY SERIES.

Crown 8vo.   3s. 6d. each volume.

By CHARLES KINGSLEY.

Westward Ho!
Yeast.
Two Years Ago.
Hereward the Wake.
The Heroes. | The Water Babies.
Madam How and Lady Why.
At Last | Prose Idylls.
Plays and Puritans, etc.
The Roman and the Teuton.
Sanitary and Social Lectures and Essays.
Historical Lectures and Essays.
Scientific Lectures and Essays.
Literary and General Lectures.
The Hermits.

Hypatia.
Alton Locke.
Glaucus: or the Wonders of The Sea-shore. With Coloured Illustrations.
Village and Town and Country Sermons.
Poems.
The Water of Life, and other Sermons.
Sermons on National Subjects, and the King of the Earth.
Sermons for the Times.
Good News of God.
The Gospel of the Pentateuch, and David.
Discipline, and other Sermons.
Westminster Sermons.
All Saints' Day, and other Sermons.

By D. CHRISTIE MURRAY.

SPECTATOR. "Mr. Christie Murray has more power and genius for the delineation of English rustic life than any half-dozen of our surviving novelists put together."

SATURDAY REVIEW.—"Few modern novelists can tell a story of English country life better than Mr. D. Christie Murray."

Aunt Rachel.
John Vale's Guardian.
Schwartz.
The Weaker Vessel.
He Fell among Thieves. D. C. MURRAY and H. HERMAN.

By Mrs. OLIPHANT.

ACADEMY.—"At her best she is, with one or two exceptions, the best of living English novelists."

SATURDAY REVIEW.—"Has the charm of style, the literary quality and flavour that never fails to please."

A Beleaguered City. | Joyce.
Neighbours on the Green.
Kirsteen. | Hester. | Sir Tom
A Country Gentleman and his Family
The Curate in Charge.
The Second Son.
He that Will Not when He May
The Railway Man and his Children.
The Marriage of Elinor.
The Heir-Presumptive and the Heir Apparent.
A Son of the Soil. | The Wizard's Son.
Young Musgrave.
Lady William

By J. H. SHORTHOUSE.

ANTI-JACOBIN "Powerful, striking, and famous romances."

John Inglesant.
Sir Percival.
The Little Schoolmaster Mark
The Countess Eve
A Teacher of the Violin
Blanche, Lady Falaise

By FREDERICK DENISON MAURICE.

Sermons Preached in Lincoln's Inn Chapel. In 6 vols.
Christmas Day, and other Sermons.
Theological Essays.
Prophets and Kings
Patriarchs and Lawgivers.
The Gospel of the Kingdom of Heaven
Gospel of St. John
Epistles of St. John
Lectures on the Apocalypse
Friendship of Books
Social Morality.
Prayer Book and Lord's Prayer
The Doctrine of Sacrifice
Acts of the Apostles

MACMILLAN AND CO., LTD., LONDON

MACMILLAN'S THREE-AND-SIXPENNY SERIES.

Crown 8vo.   3s. 6d. each volume

By CHARLOTTE M. YONGE.

The Heir of Redclyffe.
Heartsease. | Hopes and Fears.
Dynevor Terrace. | The Daisy Chain.
The Trial: More Links of the Daisy Chain.
Pillars of the House.   Vol. I.
Pillars of the House.   Vol. II.
The Young Stepmother.
The Clever Woman of the Family.
The Three Brides.
My Young Alcides. | The Caged Lion.
The Dove in the Eagle's Nest.
The Chaplet of Pearls.
Lady Hester, and the Danvers Papers.
Magnum Bonum. | Love and Life.
Unknown to History. | Stray Pearls.
The Armourer's 'Prentices.

The Two Sides of the Shield.
Nuttie's Father.
Scenes and Characters.
Chantry House.
A Modern Telemachus. | Bye-Words.
Beechcroft at Rockstone.
More Bywords.
A Reputed Changeling.
The Little Duke.
The Lances of Lynwood.
The Prince and the Page.
P's and Q's, and Little Lucy's Wonderful Globe.
Two Penniless Princesses.
That Stick.
An Old Woman's Outlook.
Grisly Grisell.

By ARCHDEACON FARRAR.

Seekers after God.
Eternal Hope. | The Fall of Man.
The Witness of History to Christ.
The Silence and Voices of God.

In the Days of thy Youth.
Saintly Workers. | Ephphatha.
Mercy and Judgment.
Sermons and Addresses in America.

By VARIOUS WRITERS.

Sir S. W. BAKER.—True Tales for My Grandsons.
W. FORBES-MITCHELL.—Reminiscences of the Great Mutiny, 1857-59.
R. BLENNERHASSETT and L. SLEEMAN.—Adventures in Mashonaland.
Sir MORTIMER DURAND, K.C.I.E.—Helen Treveryan.
'English Men of Letters' Series.   In 13 Monthly Volumes, each Volume containing three books.
LANOE FALCONER.—Cecilia de Noël.
ARCHIBALD FORBES.—Barracks, Bivouacs, and Battles.—Souvenirs of Some Continents.
W. W. FOWLER.—Tales of the Birds.   Illustrated by Bryan Hook.   A Year with the Birds.   Illustrated by Bryan Hook.
Rev. J. GILMORE.—Storm Warriors.
HENRY KINGSLEY.—Tales of Old Travel.
AMY LEVY.—Reuben Sachs.
S. R. LYSAGHT.—The Marplot.
LORD LYTTON.—The Ring of Amasis.
M. M'LENNAN.—Muckle Jock, and other Stories of Peasant Life.
LUCAS MALET.—Mrs. Lorimer.
GUSTAVE MASSON.—A French Dictionary.
A. B. MITFORD.—Tales of Old Japan.
Major G. PARRY.—The Story of Dick.
E. C. PRICE.—In the Lion's Mouth.
W. C. RHOADES.—John Trevennick.
THE WORKS OF SHAKESPEARE.   Vol. I.   Comedies.   Vol. II.   Histories.   Vol. III.   Tragedies.   3 vols.
FLORA A. STEEL.—Miss Stuart's Legacy.—The Flower of Forgiveness.
MARCHESA THEODOLI.—Under Pressure.
"TIMES" Summaries. — Biographies of Eminent Persons.   In 6 vols. — Annual Summaries.   In 2 vols.
Mrs. HUMPHRY WARD.—Miss Brethorton.
MONTAGU WILLIAMS, Q.C.—Leaves of a Life.—Later Leaves.—Round London: Down East, and Up West.
Hogan, M.P.—Tim.—The New Antigone.—Flitters, Tatters, etc.

MACMILLAN AND CO., Ltd., LONDON.

30.1.98.